THE
BLOODSTAIN

THE THIRD BLOODSTAIN

KEL RICHARDS

OM
publishing

Copyright © Beacon Communications 1995

First published in the U.K. 1996
by arrangement with Hodder Headline (Australia) Pty Limited

02 01 00 99 98 97 96   7 6 5 4 3 2 1

OM Publishing is an imprint of Paternoster Publishing,
P.O. Box 300, Carlisle, Cumbria CA3 0QS U.K.

British Library Cataloguing in Publication Data

A catalogue record for this book is available from the British Library.

ISBN 1–85078–237–7

Typeset by DOCUPRO, Sydney, Australia
Printed in Great Britain by Cox & Wyman Ltd., Reading

CHAPTER 1

After it was all over, Mark Roman thought back to how it began—before he had seen the two dead bodies and uncovered that dark cesspool of hatred and fear. It began as a talk-back call on his radio show, with no hint of the shadows the past was about to throw over the present. Such an innocent beginning.

'You know that joke of yours?' said the caller.

'Which joke?' rumbled Mark Roman, in his distinctively deep voice.

'That thing you keep saying: "Never take the blame yourself, it's always society's fault." That thing.'

'Yeah, sure.'

'Well, I know you say it just to take the micky out of people—but everyone else seems to take it seriously, and it's driving me nuts.'

'I know what you mean,' said Roman with a chuckle. 'Today nobody's at fault for anything—everyone's a victim. And if they do horrible things—well, their upbringing made them do it.'

'And they come up with the most stupid excuses!' exploded the caller on the end of the phone line. Roman took a glance at the studio clock—11:16, still 44 minutes until the show finished at midnight. Then he felt guilty about counting down the time. As a rule, nine p.m. to midnight

1

was the best part of Roman's day, but this night he wasn't enjoying his radio talk-back show as much as usual. He could feel a head cold coming on, and it was making the work of hosting the show a real effort.

'Really stupid excuses,' the caller was continuing. 'There was an article about it in this morning's *Tele-Mirror*.'

'I saw it. In fact, I clipped it out to talk about tonight,' said Roman, as he started to dig into the pile of papers on the studio console to find the newspaper clipping he wanted. If only people realised how much paper was needed to make a radio talk show, he thought to himself, as he rummaged through commercials and discarded weather forecasts.

'There was this bloke the article talked about,' the caller continued, 'who killed his wife somewhere in America—Oregon I think it said—who got off because his lawyers said he only did it to get caught! That's ridiculous, isn't it? I mean, if he did it, he's guilty. What sort of a defence is that?'

'It's what's called a "victim defence",' explained Roman. 'I've just found the clipping—let me read out the bit you were talking about. It says, let me see . . . no, it wasn't murder, it was attempted murder. Apparently he tried to kill his wife, and failed.'

'That's still a crime!'

'Of course, of course. But he was acquitted on the grounds that he suffered from something called "depression-suicide syndrome" whose victims deliberately commit poorly planned crimes with the unconscious goal of being caught or killed. His

2

defence was that he didn't *really* want to kill his wife—he *really* wanted the police to shoot him!'

'Isn't anybody guilty anymore?' wailed the caller.

'That's a good point,' rumbled Roman, and as he spoke he reached out and grabbed a thick, green book and began to shuffle rapidly through its pages.

'The word "guilt" is in my *Macquarie* on . . . here it is . . . on page 761, between "guillotine" and "guilt-complex". And *The Macquarie Dictionary* says it means "the fact or state of having committed an offence or crime." You see, there it is. If a crime or an offence has been committed, then someone is guilty of it—the person who held the gun or drove the car.'

'That's right! That's right!' squeaked the caller, excitedly. 'I knew you'd agree with me. Guilt is a real thing, isn't it?'

'It sure is. To say that I only hold up banks because daddy didn't give me enough pocket money, or I am a serial rapist because mummy didn't breastfeed me, is a lie. I put it as baldly as that. A plain lie. If you committed a crime you did it because you decided to, and you can't shift the blame onto anyone else.'

'Good on ya, Mark! You keep telling the truth, and maybe sooner or later we can get the idiots in the Government to listen to us.'

'Thanks for your call. Call again another night.'

'I'll do that. Thanks, Mark.'

As the call ended, Roman hit the start button on a cart machine, and a sharp, brassy sting of music burst into the program.

'It's now nineteen past eleven and you're listen-

3

ing to "The Mark Roman Show". If you'd like to call, there are several lines available now—so, work your fingers to the phone. Whatever's on your mind, get it off your chest. Call now.'

On those words Roman nodded at his panel operator Peter Stanley, who responded by playing the next bracket of commercials.

During the break Roman pulled out a sodden handkerchief and blew his nose twice. Then he stabbed his finger down on the intercom button and called his producer: 'Andrew—can I have another coffee please?'

Andrew Gardner's voice crackled back over the intercom, 'How's the cold?'

'Getting worse.'

'Hang in there, boss. Another forty minutes and you can go home.'

Roman was annoyed by his head cold. A head cold in winter made sense. But how could he excuse a cold in this sort of warm, autumn weather?

The call about the elimination of guilt by clever lawyers and social workers triggered off a rash of similar calls, and the subject kept the show buzzing until well after the 11:30 news headlines.

'For instance,' mused Roman in between calls, 'in America there is something called the "junk food syndrome." According to this article in today's *Tele-Mirror* a man named Dan White murdered San Fransisco mayor George Moscone, but he blamed the murder on his junk-food binges. Apparently he used to binge on sugar-rich foods, and when he did his behaviour changed. That was his defence. You see how it works: "It's not my fault. I'm not guilty. Blame it on the food I eat."

4

And the tragedy is—he got away with it. White was acquitted of murder and convicted of the lesser charge of manslaughter.'

Roman glanced up at the computer screen that kept him in touch with Andrew in the producer's room.

'Jean of Minto,' he read off the screen, 'is our next caller. Evening, Jean.'

'Good evening, Mark. And I agree absolutely with what you've been saying.'

'Good for you, Jean.'

'My daughter is doing a social-work degree at university, and she tells me that her lecturers keep saying there is no such thing as real guilt, it's just that some people suffer from a "guilt-complex". So, you see, they don't have to be punished, just cured.'

'That's it,' snapped Roman, as he dabbed his nose with his handkerchief, 'no-one's guilty, and everyone's a victim. It's one of the great lies of our age.'

'Does anyone actually admit to being guilty these days?' asked Jean. 'I mean, really admit it. To themselves, even?'

'Probably not,' agreed Roman. 'I'm sure every petty crook—and the not-so-petty crooks as well— keep telling themselves, "I'm just taking my fair share." Or something of the sort.'

'In fact, Mark,' said Jean, 'it would be interesting to know if any of your listeners actually admit to being guilty of anything.'

'Good question,' said Roman with a chuckle. 'How about you start us off, Jean? True confession time. What are you guilty of?'

The response was a musical giggle that came

5

down the phone line. 'Nothing serious, I'm afraid,' said Jean. 'I know I've done the wrong thing sometimes—snapped at poor old Ron over something that wasn't his fault. But I usually apologise afterwards. I can't pretend that I was impatient because society has treated me badly. I take responsibility for what I do.'

'Good for you, Jean. And thanks for your call.'

'Good night, Mark.'

Another commercial break got Roman two minutes closer to midnight. He gratefully sipped on the hot coffee Andrew had made for him, and it seemed to clear his head a little.

'Thirteen to twelve right now,' he said, as the commercial break ended, adding, as he checked his computer screen. 'Jeff of Chatswood is next. Evening Jeff.'

'G'day, Mark. I wanted to follow up on what Jean was saying.'

'Sure.'

'That is to say . . . well . . . there still are some of us who know what it means to be guilty. We don't try to palm off the blame onto junk foods or booze, even if we'd had a bit to drink at the time. The problem is . . . if you are guilty, what do you do about it?'

'Explain what you mean, Jeff.'

'Well . . . what I'm saying is that I **feel** guilty about something that happened years ago.'

'Something serious?'

'Yeah. Pretty serious. And I've felt guilty about it for all this time. I suppose those social-work lecturers would say that I have a "guilt-complex" and I need to be cured. But I don't think I have

6

any sort of complex. I think I really *am* guilty! But what can I do about it?'

'You want to get rid of your feelings of guilt?'

'Not just the feelings. I want to get rid of the guilt itself—the real guilt. I've had nightmares about it. They still come back sometimes, even after all these years. I want the guilt feelings to go away. But I think that will only happen if I can do something about the guilt itself. But I don't know what.'

This call was provoking in Roman the ambivalent feelings that such calls often did. On the one hand, he really wanted to help this young man (at least, his voice sounded young on the phone line). On the other hand, there was part of his mind that said, 'This is great radio—keep it going!' And Roman felt guilty of exploitation whenever that thought shot into his mind.

'Do you want to tell us what it is you did, all those years ago?' asked Roman, as gently as he could.

'I . . . well, it was something . . . that is . . .' For a split second Jeff came close to telling his whole story, and then the moment passed. 'No . . . no, I don't think I could. I just feel so awful about it that to admit it out loud is . . . just impossible.'

'Alright then,' continued Roman gently. 'Then tell me this. We are talking about something that you **did**—right?'

'Yes, that's right.'

'Not recently, but some years ago?'

'Yes.'

'Was someone hurt by what you did?'

'Yes.'

'Badly hurt?'

7

'Yes.'

'More than one person?'

'In a sense, yes, I guess that more than one person always ends up being hurt.'

'And you know for sure that what happened was your fault?'

'Yes.'

'Have you ever told anyone?'

'No. No. I tried once, but I just couldn't get it out.'

'Maybe telling someone would help?'

'It might help my feelings—my "guilt-complex"—but it won't do anything about the guilt, the thing itself. What can I do about that?'

'Okay, let's look at that. Is the person you hurt, still alive?'

'Yes.'

'Do you know where this victim is? Could you make contact?'

'I do now. Yes, I could.'

'Then here's my advice: ask the victim to forgive you.'

'Forgive me?'

'At the very heart of dealing with guilt, real responsible guilt, is the notion of forgiveness.'

'Ah, I see.' Suddenly the caller's voice sounded flat, and disappointed. 'And that's it?'

'Forgiveness is bigger and more powerful than you can see at this moment, Jeff,' insisted Roman.

'Well, I'll think about your advice. Maybe I'll call you back later. Thanks, Mark.'

As the call disappeared with a clunk, Roman punched a button and played one of his softer, longer, music bridges. When it ended he said, 'I wish I could get Jeff to take the notion of forgiveness more seriously. In some cases we can pay for the damage we have done, in other cases we can't. And those are the hard ones. If Jeff's guilt won't go away, it's because that guilt has never been forgiven. And in most cases where forgiveness is a problem, there is no way that the offender—in this case, Jeff—can put things right. But that just makes forgiveness all the more important.'

And that triggered a series of calls on forgiveness. None of them were very helpful. There were some callers who wanted to boast about how they had forgiven some terrible wrong that had been done to them. And others who wanted to insist that some things can just never be forgiven.

'What sort of things can never be forgiven?' Roman asked 'Reg of Pymble.'

'Torture. Deliberate cruelty. That sort of thing,' he replied, with an angry snarl.

'Interesting you should say that,' returned Roman, putting some steel into his deep voice, 'because last Anzac Day on this show I interviewed an old Aussie bloke who had been a POW. Held by the Japanese at Changi. And he said on this show that he had forgiven the Japanese for what they did to him. He still had scars on his back from the torture—but he had forgiven them.'

'Yeah, well, maybe some people can forgive, and some can't,' snapped the caller.

'Or maybe some will and some won't,' replied Roman. 'Thanks for your call,' he added as he closed the phone fader so that Reg could not get another word in. Tonight Roman didn't have the energy to cope with an angry, argumentative caller.

There was one last commercial break, and then Roman was wrapping up the show.

9

'Don't forget,' he reminded his listeners, 'that tomorrow afternoon at two o'clock I'll be doing the official opening of an art exhibition at the Chatswood Civic Centre. The exhibition has been organised by Rotary to raise money for children with leukaemia, so it's a worthy cause. All the paintings are by Aussie bush artists, and they are all for sale. So I'll see you tomorrow afternoon at two. And I'll be back here at the usual time of nine o'clock on Monday night. Have a good weekend. Good night, and God bless.'

With that he closed the mic switch and faded up his famous theme music to play out to the pips.

As the news theme started after the midnight time signal Andrew walked into the studio, and said with a sympathetic smile, 'Well, you survived that, Mark. The head cold turned out not to be fatal after all.'

'Not yet,' growled Roman. 'Just you wait. With any luck I'll be dead by Monday.'

'Do I get to do the show on Monday night then?' said his producer with a cheeky grin.

'Would you like to do a dying man a favour?' mumbled Roman as he pushed his bulky frame out of the studio chair.

'Sure. What favour?'

'Clean up this mess in the studio, throw out all the bits of paper that we've finished with, put the rest in my office and lock up.'

'No problem.'

Andrew Gardner was tall, thin, and red-haired. And he seemed to have an endless source of cheerful energy.

'You get straight home, Mark, and take that cold of yours to bed.'

Roman walked to the lifts with his distinctive heavy tread. He was not a fat man, just tall and solidly built, but he had the walk of a much heavier man. The lift carried him down to the car park in the basement of the radio station, where his aging, green Volvo was parked in the spot marked with his name.

As he drove home through the mild, still night air, Roman found himself thinking about Jeff's call and his lack of belief in the power of forgiveness. Roman shook his head sadly at the extent to which people seemed to misunderstand how the world worked, and what really mattered.

When he arrived home at his apartment building in McDougall Street, Milsons Point, he found a parking spot next to Milson Park, and walked with slow, weary steps to his front door. Stepping inside his second-floor apartment, he pressed a switch and flooded the place with warm, yellow light. But, for once, it did not feel like home—like the warm, snug burrow he came back to every night after the show.

That was because he lived alone. As a solitary, self-contained man, most of the time he accepted this in an almost contented fashion. But when illness struck—even something as minor as a head cold—he felt cheated by his lonely lifestyle. Closing the apartment door, he instinctively looked at the mantelpiece and the photograph of Linda nursing young Sharon. They had died in a car accident nearly three years ago. The hurt had largely healed. But as Roman blew his nose, he wanted Linda back again, to fuss over him and nurse him. He wanted little Sharon back to give him a hug 'to make Daddy better.'

11

He roused himself from these unhelpful feelings and turned on the BBC World Service radio for company. Resisting the temptation to do nothing, to just sink down into an armchair or onto the bed, he forced himself to a sensible routine. He found a bottle of 500-ml vitamin C tablets, and washed half a dozen of them down with orange juice. He heated up a can of Campbell's tomato soup, and made himself eat two large bowls full. Then he had a long, hot, luxurious shower, tumbled into bed, and fell asleep almost at once.

The next morning, when Roman woke he checked his bedside clock and found that it was almost ten o'clock. An hour after his usual waking time. He took a deep breath through his nostrils. Clear. Perhaps the head cold had come and gone in just twenty-four hours?

Feeling cheered by this prospect, Roman climbed out of bed and padded out to the kitchen. He took a couple of par-baked bread rolls out of their packet in the fridge, and put them into his fan-forced oven to cook. At the same time he filled up the coffee dripolator and turned it on. These preparations made, he had a shower, and dressed for the day.

To be on the safe side, he took another handful of vitamin C tablets, and sat down to his breakfast of hot rolls and coffee. Usually his first task every morning was to walk up to the Milsons Point shops to buy a newspaper, but enough of the virus was still in Roman's system to make him feel tired and lethargic. He couldn't be bothered with the walk, and so occupied himself over breakfast with one of Christine Lovatt's *Colossus Crossword* magazines in place of the newspaper.

Then he tidied up his kitchen, and, with some reluctance, tackled his regular Saturday morning chores; he vacuumed and swept and dusted, and mopped the kitchen and bathroom floors.

The work done, he pulled an armchair into a pool of sunlight near the front window and promptly fell asleep. It was just after 12 when he woke with a start. Blinking in confusion, he tried to remember. There was something he had to do today, what was it? A moment later it came back to him—the official opening of the art show at Chatswood. That was it. In less than two hours' time.

'The only way to keep going is to keep going,' he said to himself. With this thought in mind, he locked up the apartment and drove his old green Volvo to Chatswood. After crawling through a hovering swarm of cars for what felt like an hour, Roman finally succeeded in parking his car in the council car park behind Grace Brothers.

He filled in the time before the art show opening by eating lunch at Pizza Hut and by doing some slow, ambling window-shopping through Grace Brothers, Westfield, Chatswood Chase and Lemon Grove. Eventually, at a few minutes to two, he made his way to the Chatswood Civic Centre.

There was already a large crowd walking around the hall, looking at the paintings. For a moment he stood in the entrance feeling a little lost, and then he heard a voice calling him.

'Mark! So glad you could make it!'

Roman turned around to see Leon Blake hurrying towards him. Leon was the local Rotary organiser. He was a short, round man, with a military moustache and a large, warm smile.

'How are you, Mark? Keeping well?' was the

greeting that accompanied a handshake like a hydraulic pump.

'Not too badly. Yesterday I was coming down with a head cold but, knock on wood, I seem to have shaken it off.'

'Good. Good. Not good that you got it, but good that you got rid of it. Come and I'll introduce you to the other members of the committee.'

Roman spent the next few minutes forcing a pleasant smile onto his face (at least, he imagined it was pleasant—how it looked to others he had no idea), and listening to the same things people always said when they met him.

'I love your radio show, Mr Roman.'

'I listen every single night.'

'It must be great fun to do that show of yours.'

They were just being polite, but today Mark's patience was thin and he felt he'd heard it all before.

'I'll have to drag Mark away from you folks now,' said Leon, taking Roman by the elbow and steering him towards a platform at the end of the room where he was placed in a chair between the mayor and a local doctor who was also the district governor of Rotary.

Leon Blake chaired the opening, and did so with enthusiasm and a slick, professional manner. The mayor 'said a few words,' and then the governor did the same. Eventually Roman was summoned to do his thing. He told a few jokes about amusing incidents that had occurred on his radio show, praised the paintings as being realistic portrayals of the Aussie bush 'not the abstract rubbish that gets palmed off as art these days,' and eventually declared the exhibition and sale to be officially

14

open. The crowd in the hall applauded loudly, and Roman began to relax, his duty done.

'Now, come and have some drinks and canapés with the committee,' Leon Blake said as they stepped down from the platform. Roman was about to follow Blake when he felt a tug on his sleeve.

He turned around and found himself facing a man in his mid-thirties, his good looks spoiled by the anxious expression on his face.

'May I have a word with you, please, Mr Roman?' he asked.

'You go on, Leon,' said Roman, 'I'll join you later.'

'Righty-ho. I'll tell the others you're coming,' said Leon heartily, as he waded off through the crowd.

'Now, what can I do for you?' asked Roman, turning back to the young man.

'I spoke to you last night on your radio show,' he said.

'Oh, yes?'

'I'm Jeff of Chatswood. Do you remember? I asked you about dealing with guilt.'

'Ah, yes, of course. I remember your call very well.'

'I was wondering if I could have a talk with you at some time.'

'What about?' asked Roman suspiciously.

'About what you were saying. You know. About forgiveness dealing with guilt.'

'Yes, of course. I'd be happy to talk to you about it.'

'Could I come back when you've finished at this reception, or whatever you're going to?'

'Why don't we talk now?' suggested Roman.

15

… Mr proved that he had made good friends all
window bead he than the little auto, pad
a show some toad new, about her in a smoker
windows some of the new about as they
steps a little the park must as a short
so pellet. Handmade he read there, his about
a he news about wed d, from, tome the eyes
was in its and made, also must in a smoker in

CHAPTER 2

'Now,' said Roman, once they were seated at a
quiet corner table in a coffee shop at the entrance
to Westfield Shopping Centre, 'do you want to tell
me the rest of your name, or do you want to go
on being Jeff-from-Chatswood?'

'Ottway—Jeff Ottway's my name, Mr Roman
. . .'

'Please, call me Mark, everyone does,' Roman
interrupted, as he tried to get the sugar through the
foam and into the coffee.

'Mark, then. I must admit that I feel like I know
you—just through listening to the radio show.'

'How can I help you? What did you want to talk
about?'

'About this idea that forgiveness is the cure for
guilt. It sounded like a daft idea when you first
said it. But I've been thinking about it since. And
I . . . well, I guess I want you to tell me more
about it . . . because . . .'

'Because this guilt is really bothering you?'

'Exactly! It's been such a long time. I keep
expecting that it will go away, but it doesn't. It's
like a heavy burden on my shoulders. And I just
can't carry the weight much longer. So tell me
about forgiveness.'

'Well, to start with—the normal human response
to hurt is anger on the part of the person who gets

hurt, and guilt on the part of the person who did the hurting. That's normal. The only people who don't feel any guilt at all after hurting someone are the psychopaths. In fact, that's almost a definition of what "psychopath" means.'

'So—I'm normal then?' said Ottway, with the slightest of smiles—the first time Roman had seen anything even remotely resembling a smile on his grim face.

'Yes, normal. Mind you, lots of normal people suppress the signals of guilt that their conscience sends them.'

'I wish I could do that!' muttered Ottway bitterly.

'It's healthier if you don't—if you face the guilt and deal with it. Now the next step: do you think that you could apologise to the person, or persons, you have hurt?'

'Apologise?'

'Exactly.'

'The trouble is . . . well, when a hurt is a big one, and an on-going one, an apology seems so lame.'

'Sure. "Sorry" is not a magic formula. It should not prevent us from talking about real problems and looking for real solutions. But "sorry", a real, genuine "sorry", can be a major part of those solutions. Do you think you could do that?'

There was a long silence, and Roman was about to ask the question a second time, when Jeff Ottway spoke.

'I think I could,' he said slowly, 'I'm not dead sure. But I think I could. It would be very hard. But then . . . Let me think about it.'

'Another part of this process is seeing things from the other person's point of view. If you can

17

imagine what it's like to be them, to walk in their shoes, that will help.'

'How?'

'You will need to find the willpower not only to confess your guilt to the person, or persons, you have hurt, but also to let them know that you have some understanding of what they have been through, and that you are genuinely sorry.'

'That sounds hard.'

'It is hard. If it was easy, more people would do it.'

'I just wish I was rich.'

'Rich?' said Roman, surprised. 'Why rich?'

'Then I could pay compensation. And that would clear it all up.'

'Perhaps it would. And perhaps it wouldn't. The great myth of the age we live in is that money fixes everything. There are lots of things that can only be fixed by honesty, confession, love, and what I would call "other-centredness"—if that makes sense to you?'

'But,' said Ottway, his face as twisted with anxiety as ever, 'where do I find the will to confront, and confess, and say "Sorry" . . . where do I get that?'

'Well,' replied Roman, 'my answer is that God . . .'.

'Leave God out of this!' interrupted Ottway quickly.

'Do you really imagine that you can leave God out of anything?' asked Roman, using his deepest radio voice.

'Thanks for your advice, Mr Roman,' said Ottway, pushing back his chair and rising from the table, 'I'll think about it.'

18

With that he turned on his heels and walked out of the coffee shop. Roman went to the counter and paid for the two cappuccinos, and then walked thoughtfully back onto the street.

Outside the sky was cloudless, and, even though it was autumn, the temperature was back into the high twenties again. Suddenly, a stab of guilty conscience shot through Roman. He had promised Leon Blake that he would attend the reception as soon as he had dealt with Jeff Ottway. He was tempted to sneak back home, but a promise was a promise.

Roman stumped across Victoria Avenue, weaving in and out of the stationary cars waiting for the lights to change, and up the steps of the Chatswood Civic Centre.

As he entered the building he was approached by a young woman with a badge saying 'Willougby Council' on her jacket.

'Mr Roman?'

Roman nodded.

'I was asked to wait for you here and take you up to the reception in the mayor's chambers when you came back.'

The good news for Roman was that as he arrived the reception was within ten minutes of ending. The bad news was that he still had a soggy canapé thrust into one hand, and a glass of warm white wine out of a plastic cask thrust into the other. Then he was whisked around the room to meet various civic dignitaries with whom he could not shake hands, since both hands were full.

Leon Blake was genuinely grateful that he had come back to be trotted around the room like a trophy, so, as Roman made his way back to the car park he felt the warm inner glow that comes from having kept a promise.

Back in his apartment Roman took more vitamin C tablets, and some panadol for the sore throat that was just developing, and steamed his head underneath a towel draped over a basin full of boiling water and Vicks VapoRub.

Then he changed into his pyjamas, lay down on his bed and, much to his surprise, fell asleep again.

The next morning he again woke late, but feeling quite recovered—except for a mouth ulcer, which was now making its presence felt. But Roman was still cautious—he knew the cold virus was hanging around somewhere just waiting for the chance to spring back at him. Nevertheless, Roman decided he was well enough for his regular Sunday routine.

This always started with washing. Roman's 'laundry' was nothing more than a cupboard in one corner of his bathroom. When the slatted wooden door of this cupboard was opened it revealed a front-opening washing machine, and, fixed to the wall above it, a clothes drier. Roman loaded the washing machine with bedlinen and everything from the dirty clothes basket, and set its automatic cycle running.

Then he drove to Neutral Bay to put his old green Volvo through the car-wash, as he did every Sunday morning. The staff provided him with a free cup of coffee, and, as always, he bought a newspaper, the *Sunday Telegraph*, there. While the car was being pulled through the sprays and the spinning brushes he opened the paper and turned first, as he always did, to the radio column. Tۃ ing nothing of interest there, he turned back to the front page, and started to read the paper through in an orderly fashion.

From the car-wash he drove to the Cremorne deli where he had breakfast every Sunday—usually bagels and smoked salmon with cottage cheese—eaten while he finished reading the paper.

The rest of Sunday consisted of the head cold trying to reassert itself, and Roman doctoring himself with whatever came to hand in an attempt to beat back its advances. When Sunday night came, Roman wasn't sure whether he was well enough to go to church or not. But he knew that if he stayed home he would just feel miserable—so he went.

Conveniently for Roman, the minister of St Thomas' Anglican Church at North Sydney, Hugh Marsden, preached that night on forgiveness. Roman sat in his pew busily scribbling down notes from what Hugh was saying. He felt certain that, following Friday's discussion, forgiveness was bound to come up again on the open line as a talk-back topic. And he also felt that he needed all the material he could gather to explain the role of forgiveness to Jeff Ottway.

Roman didn't hang around after church socialising, as he usually did—instead he took his cold home and tucked it into bed.

On Monday morning Roman woke at his usual time, and, apart from a nagging mouth ulcer, felt completely well. He walked up to the shops at Milsons Point to buy the Monday edition of the *Daily Telegraph-Mirror*, which he read over his usual breakfast of hot rolls and coffee.

At lunchtime he went to the Crows Nest Club to

eat lunch and play snooker with one of his friends from the radio station, Jack Kingston.

'What do you get if you cross a parrot with a tiger?' demanded Kingston, when Roman found him in the club bar.

'I have no idea, Jack,' said Roman. He liked Kingston enormously, but occasionally wished he would stop performing. 'I don't know what you get if you cross a parrot with a tiger.'

'I don't know either,' replied Kingston, 'but if it says "Polly wants a cracker" you'd damn well better feed it!'

'When are you going to publish your joke book, Jack?'

'Funny you should ask that. I'm having lunch with a publisher later this week, to see if I can sell them on the idea.'

'I hope the lunch goes well, then. In the meantime—how about our lunch?'

'You lead the way, while I order drinks.'

Roman found a table in the dining room, and Kingston joined him a few minutes later, bearing two large glasses of Coke.

'Jack, there's something I want to ask your advice about,' said Roman, after the meals had been served, and they had both begun to eat.

'Ask the oracle. The massive depths of my wisdom are at your command,' replied Kingston.

Roman told Kingston about his meeting with Jeff Ottway, about Ottway's problem (or as much as he knew of it) and about the advice he had given.

'Well,' he said at the end of his story, 'what do you think?'

'I think that so far, what you've told this bloke

is safe enough. But if you want my advice—you should stop.'

'Stop?'

'Precisely. Don't get involved in the lives of your listeners. We entertain them. We do radio shows for them. If they need counselling, let them go to someone who's qualified. It's very dangerous to get involved in listeners' lives. You don't know what it might lead to.'

'I have a bit of an idea,' said Roman, with heavy irony in his voice.

'Yes, of course you do,' replied Kingston, 'and that's exactly my point. Last time you got involved in the lives of listeners you found a dead body, and wound up in the middle of a murder investigation. Leave it alone, Mark—that's my advice.'

That night on his talk-back show the callers once again raised the subject of forgiveness. They were especially keen to tell the world just exactly what they could and could not forgive.

'Beverly of Baulkham Hills is on the line,' said Roman, reading the information off his computer screen. 'Evening, Bev.'

'Good evening, Mark.'

'Do you prefer Beverly, or Bev?'

'Just Bev, please. That's what everyone calls me.'

'Okay. Now, what did you want to talk about?'

'On Friday night—late in the show—you were talking about forgiveness. Remember?'

'I do indeed.'

'Well, I was thinking about it all over the week-end. And I think that if someone raped me, that is just such a horrible violation that I could never forgive them.'

'Would it surprise you to learn that some people have?'

'Have what?'

'Forgiven rapists. And worse.'

'It would surprise me. It would astonish me. I just don't understand it.'

'Well, let me give you a concrete example,' said Roman, reaching for the notes he had made the night before, during Hugh Marsden's sermon. 'For instance, back in 1986 three men broke into a home in West London, searching for money. Finding nothing of value, they became violent. Two of them brutally raped the daughter of the house. Her boyfriend and father were tied up and beaten with a baseball bat.'

'How could anyone ever forgive that?'

'Well,' continued Roman, 'this particular family was a Christian family and they did. Their immediate reaction was to forgive. In a radio interview the girl said, "At the time it happened forgiveness was natural. Later I had to work it out. I knew that not forgiving would destroy me." Can you understand that?'

'I can sort of understand,' said the caller. 'She's saying that she's forgiving them for her own sake—so that she doesn't get eaten up by anger, or something like that.'

'Yes, that's true,' said Roman. 'But I think she's saying more than that. Anyway, let me finish the story. Eleven months later the three men were in court, and the judge gave much lighter sentences for the rape than for the robbery. The judge said the family had overcome their ordeal so well that the victim's suffering couldn't have been too bad.'

'Stupid judges!' interrupted Bev.

'You won't get an argument from me about that!' agreed Roman. 'Anyway, the father protested strongly about the unjust sentences.'

'Well, that's a contradiction, isn't it? How can he forgive them and still want them punished?'

'I'm not sure,' admitted Roman. 'It's a bit of a puzzler, isn't it? If we forgive someone, does that mean that the full force of the law should no longer apply?'

That was enough to make the switchboard light up like a Christmas tree. Everyone had an opinion on that, and it took the next two hours to get through most of the calls.

Then, shortly after the eleven–thirty p.m. news headlines, Roman noticed the name 'Jeff of Chatswood' on his computer screen.

'What does he want?' he asked Andrew over the intercom.

'He says it's a follow-up to Friday night's call,' explained Andrew.

'Okay,' said Roman, 'I'll take it next.'

A minute later a commercial break came to an end. 'Coming up,' Peter Stanley's voice crackled over the intercom, 'out words: "at a store near you." In fifteen.'

Fifteen seconds later Roman heard the cue words, punched the flashing button on his open line board, and said, 'Jeff of Chatswood is next. Evening, Jeff.'

'Evening, Mark. I'm calling about the same subject I rang about on Friday night.'

'For those who weren't listening on Friday—Jeff rang to say that he had deep feelings of guilt about something in his past, and he wanted to know how to deal with that guilt.'

25

'And you said that forgiveness would deal with it,' added Jeff.

'Yes, that's right, I did.'

'And on Saturday afternoon, you said I should apologise.'

'I'd better explain to the listeners,' interrupted Roman, 'that Jeff and I met at the opening of the art show in Chatswood on Saturday afternoon. We talked about Jeff's problem again, and what he says is quite right. I suggested that he apologise, and see what sort of reaction he got. Did you try it, Jeff?'

'Yes, I did. Yesterday afternoon.'

'Did it achieve anything?'

'No. Nothing. It was a terrible experience. The person I apologised to sort of went bananas—and yelled abuse at me. It was just awful.'

'I'm sorry it worked out so badly for you, Jeff. Did you try to convey that you understood the hurt this person had suffered?'

'Yes I did. But I wasn't listened to.'

'Well, if you have genuinely and sincerely tried to apologise, and you weren't listened to, then perhaps you have done all that you can do.'

'What do you mean?'

'I mean that if your apology has been rejected, then perhaps that is reason enough to say that you are no longer guilty.'

'Do you really think so?'

'I'm still working this through as I'm saying it,' said Roman. 'But look here: is there any way that you could compensate this person for the hurt they have suffered?'

'I . . . I don't think so . . . no, I'm not sure.'

'If you had stolen something, then you could

return it,' rumbled Roman in the deep voice that had made him a radio star. 'Is it anything like that?'

'No, nothing like that. It wasn't that kind of thing at all.'

'So if there is no compensation that you can provide, and if your attempts at a genuine, sincere and humble apology have been rejected, then perhaps you now have no further reason to feel guilty. Or to actually *be* guilty.'

'I see,' said Jeff, somewhat doubtfully.

'I'd be interested to hear what other listeners think about that. Why don't we leave it there for now, Jeff? You go back to your radio, and see what other people have to say?'

'Okay. I'll call you again later, Mark.'

'Good night, Jeff.'

Roman hit a station jingle, and then invited more calls—especially people who had some thoughts to share on Jeff's problem.

When the program ended at midnight, Roman packed up his papers and files that were scattered around the studio and took them back to the tiny office the radio station provided for him. He had been sitting at his desk for a few minutes when the phone rang. It was his producer, Andrew Gardner.

'I have a caller on line one for you, Mark. His name is Jeff Ottway. He says he knows you. Do you want to take the call?'

Roman heaved a deep sigh, and hesitated for a moment.

'I'd better talk to him,' he said at last.

'Putting him through,' said Andrew.

There was a click on the line, and then Jeff

Ottway's voice could be heard, 'Mark, are you there?'

'Yes, I'm here, Jeff.'

'I'm sorry to disturb you off the air, but I really need a chance to talk to you about what happened when I took your advice. It was pretty horrible. Vicious even.'

'I'm sorry my advice got you into that sort of situation.'

'Oh, I'm not blaming you, Mark,' said Jeff. 'Don't get me wrong. I can understand now that what you said is dead right. The question is: how do you handle it when someone doesn't want to be apologised to?'

'That's a tough one,' Roman rumbled into the telephone, 'and I'm not sure I'm qualified to handle it. Would you like me to get you the name of a good counsellor—someone you can talk all of this over with?'

'No. I'm sorry if I sound ungrateful. It's just that this is really personal stuff. And very heavy. And, like I said on Saturday, I feel that you're a friend—a mate. I know you through the radio, and I can talk to you. I don't think I could talk to anyone else.'

'Well, if that's how you feel, I'm happy to talk to you. I just don't know if I can be of any use, that's all.'

'That's terrific, Mark. If we could just meet again. This is not something I can discuss over the phone. You could come to my place, or I could call in to your place?'

'No,' interrupted Roman quickly. The last thing he wanted was people invading the sanctuary of his home. 'I'll drop into your place, Jeff. Just give me an address and a time.'

'I live in a block of units in Cambridge Street— 12 Cambridge Street, Chatswood, unit four.'

'And a time?'

'Well, I'm on shift work at the moment. In fact, I leave for work in about an hour. And I'll be back home again at ten in the morning. Could you call around then?'

'At ten a.m.? Sure, if that suits you.'

'My wife and daughter are away visiting Caitlin's parents down at Wagga at the moment— so there's just me here, and we can have a private chat.'

'Alright. Tomorrow morning, or, rather, this morning, since it's after midnight, at ten o'clock. I'll see you then.'

The minute Roman put the phone down he had serious qualms about whether he had done the right thing or not. He remembered Jack Kingston's strong advice. But this was a cry for help, and he couldn't ignore it.

CHAPTER 3

Number 12 Cambridge Street turned out to be one of those tall narrow blocks of home units. Roman estimated it to be ten storeys high. It stood among a group of similar blocks. At precisely ten a.m. Roman parked near the corner of Cambridge and High, and walked through the buttery-soft sunshine to the building. It was surrounded by neatly manicured lawns, and small, flower-filled garden beds of almost mathematical precision.

The front glass door was one of those security affairs, and beside it was an arrangement of grilles and buttons that allowed you to talk to whoever you had come to visit. As Roman reached over to press number four, the door was opened from inside by a woman dressed in a business suit who rushed out in a great hurry. Roman grabbed the door before it could swing closed, and let himself into the building without needing to use the security intercom.

He found himself in a broad, carpeted corridor punctuated at regular intervals by solid timber doors and by occasional glass panels letting in sunlight from the garden. The first door Roman came to was numbered 'One.' 'Four' turned out to be the last of them, at the end of the corridor.

Roman knocked gently. There was no response. He waited for a full minute, then knocked again more firmly—this time the strength of his knocking was enough to cause the door to swing inwards. Roman was surprised.

'Jeff? Jeff Ottway? Are you there, Jeff?'

He pushed the door fully open, and called again.

'Jeff? It's Mark Roman. Are you there?'

Silence was the only response, giving Roman a sinking feeling in his stomach.

He advanced a step or two into the unit, then stopped and called again.

'Jeff?' For some reason, he was speaking softly now, his voice almost hushed. 'Jeff? Are you around?'

He was standing in a small hallway. Roman advanced another half a dozen steps. At the end of the hall, the room opened out. There was a small, round, dining table with four chairs. Beyond was a lounge area, with a sofa and armchairs, and a coffee table standing between them. Beyond that was a floor-to-ceiling glass window. Or, more likely, a sliding glass door, Roman realised.

He walked past the dining table, and then stopped abruptly. He had found Jeff Ottway—lying on the carpet, face upwards, eyes closed, a dark bloodstain underneath his head. Roman knelt down beside the body and picked up a pale, limp wrist. Not only was there no pulse, it was quite cold. Jeff Ottway had been dead for some time.

Roman felt a cold wave of fear wash over him—that inexplicable fear we feel in the presence of death.

He stood up and looked around for a telephone. He found it sitting on a breakfast bar that jutted out of the kitchen nook in one corner of the room. Roman had picked up the receiver and started to dial 000, when he had a better idea. Beside the phone was a phone book. He looked up the number of Chatswood Police Station, and dialled it.

'Chatswood Police.'

'I'd like to report a murder.'

'Can I have your name please, sir, and your address.'

'My name is Mark Roman . . .'

'Oh, yes—I recognise the voice!' interrupted the police officer on the end of the phone.

'. . . and I'm standing in unit four, number 12, Cambridge Street, Chatswood. I've just arrived to keep an appointment, and I've found the man I was to meet lying dead on the floor.'

'Murdered?'

'There's blood around his head. I don't see how it could be anything else.'

'Could the perpetrators still be on the premises, Mr Roman?'

'The body is cold to the touch. So, I'd say that's unlikely.'

'We'll have some people with you in just a couple of minutes, Mr Roman. Just stay there, and don't touch anything.'

Roman hung up the telephone, and slowly looked around the room.

It was a very ordinary-looking room. Sitting on top of a stereo, on the opposite wall, was a coloured photo of a dark-haired woman who might have been in her mid-twenties. Standing beside her was a fair-haired girl of perhaps three or four years of age.

Roman walked across the room, being careful to step well away from the body. He came to the glass door and looked out. A small garden ran from the back of the building to a paling fence, perhaps no more than four metres away. Near the glass door stood some outdoor furniture. Beyond, well-manicured grass rose in a gentle slope to the fence.

He looked back again at the body. As well as the congealing blood under the head, there was a long smear running from the glass sliding door, across the carpet, to where the body lay.

Jeff Ottway had died wearing a uniform of some sort. Or, perhaps, 'overalls' would be a better description. The word 'Comtel' was stitched onto the pocket. Presumably that was the company he worked for.

Roman was startled out of his meditations by a severe buzzing on the wall near his ear. He pressed the intercom button.

'Yes?'

'Police here. Is that Mr Roman?'

'Yes it is.'

'Release the security lock please, Mr Roman, and let us in.'

Roman pressed the button marked 'Open Door'. A moment later two plain-clothes police officers entered the room, followed by two uniformed men.

'I'm Detective Marsh, Mr Roman, and this is Detective McDermott.'

'Hello,' said Roman, rather weakly. Well, he thought, what do you say to a policeman at the scene of a murder?

'When did you arrive, Mr Roman?' continued Marsh after taking a brief look at the body.

'Ten minutes ago, I guess. Certainly no more than that. I was due here at ten o'clock, and I was running about on time.'

Marsh glanced at his wristwatch. This prompted Roman to look at the clock on the wall opposite. It said twelve minutes past ten. It was one of those clocks with a polished timber face and gold numerals, with metallic, gold-coloured spikes sticking out from it at the twelve, three, six and nine positions.

'How did you get in?'

'The door was unlocked. It started to swing open when I knocked on it, so I called out and came in.'

'Yes, but how did you get into the building? How did you get past the security at the front door? Did someone press the button from inside this unit and let you in?' It was the other detective, McDermott, who asked these questions.

'No,' explained Roman. 'There was a woman coming out, so I just walked in while the door was still open.'

'These security systems are useless!' snorted McDermott.

'What's the dead man's name, Mr Roman?' asked Marsh.

'Jeff Ottway.'

'How well did you know him?'

'Hardly at all.'

'So what was your connection with him then?'

'He came to me for advice.'

'He must have been pretty hard up for advice!' muttered McDermott, just loudly enough to be heard. This earned a scowl from Marsh, who seemed to be the senior officer.

'Check out the other rooms, Don,' said Marsh, and McDermott left.

'Jim Kline is a mate of mine, Mr Roman.'

'I remember Detective Kline,' replied Roman. 'He impressed me as a good policeman.'

'And he told me that you impressed him as a good citizen, so any help you can give in the matter of this death I'm sure you will . . .'

'Of course!'

'. . . but just because you became involved in the solution to the Escobar murder case, I don't want you getting strange ideas and playing amateur detective on me. Okay, Mr Roman?'

'I'm more than happy to leave detecting to the professionals. And, please, call me, Mark—everyone does.'

'Policemen aren't comfortable doing that, so, if you won't take offence, I'll stick to "Mr Roman." Okay?'

'Of course.'

At this point McDermott strutted back into the room.

'Nothing anywhere else,' he reported. 'There's two bedrooms—main and a child's—and a bathroom, and that's it. No sign of a struggle, or of any disturbance.'

'Thanks, Don,' said Marsh. 'Would you wait by the front door, and let in the scientific blokes when they arrive?'

McDermott disappeared again.

'So, you were about to tell me your connection with the deceased.'

It sent a shiver down Roman's spine to hear Jeff Ottway referred to as 'the deceased.'

'He called my radio show to talk about a problem he had.'

'What sort of problem?'

'He was carrying a burden of guilt. Something

35

to do with some hurt he had inflicted on a person. Quite a few years ago, I gather. He never explained exactly what. He wanted advice on how to handle the feelings of guilt. Or, rather, the guilt itself.'

'And that was the only contact?'

'No. He spoke to me at the Chatswood Civic Centre on Saturday afternoon. I was opening an art show there. He came up and introduced himself, and wanted to continue the conversation. Which we did. But he didn't tell me very much more in the way of details.'

'And what advice did you give him?'

'I told him to confront the person he had hurt. To confess, and apologise, and ask for forgiveness.'

'Did he?'

'He said he tried. But he was rebuffed.'

'And when did he report this to you?'

'He rang the show last night. And then he spoke to me again off-air, just after midnight. He wanted more advice and asked me to call and see him. At ten o'clock this morning. That's how I came to be here.'

'You wouldn't happen to know whether he has any family, would you?'

'He mentioned a wife and daughter—said they were on holidays, visiting her parents. Now, where did he say? Ah, yes—in Wagga.'

'That's very helpful, Mr Roman. You didn't catch her name, did you? It'll be here in the unit somewhere, but if you know . . .'

'He called her "Caitlin" when he was talking to me on the phone last night. But, of course, I don't know what her maiden name was.'

'You've been very helpful, Mr Roman. If you

36

don't have to rush off anywhere, I'd like you to hang around for a little while. Just until we've done the basic physical examination of the scene. Then I might ask you one or two more questions. Is that a problem?'

'No, of course not.'

'Perhaps you'd prefer to wait in one of the bedrooms?' suggested Marsh.

'Actually,' said Roman, 'I'd rather get a breath of fresh air, if that's alright with you?'

Marsh looked at Roman quizzically for a moment, and then said, 'Okay.'

The detective went over to the glass door, and, using his handkerchief so as not to spoil any fingerprints, checked the catch. It slid back in response to his gentle tug—clearly it had not been locked.

Before he allowed Roman outside, the detective stepped outside himself and looked around the small backyard.

'You can come out, Mr Roman,' called Marsh.

Roman stepped out onto the grass.

'You can wait here. Take a seat if you wish,' added Marsh, gesturing at the outdoor furniture. Then he went back inside.

Roman took a seat. For a moment he sat, staring into space, assimilating all that had happened. When he looked up, he found one of the uniformed policemen was standing near the back door.

Keeping an eye on me, thought Roman to himself. Does that mean I am a suspect in this murder?

CHAPTER 4

Cars could be heard pulling up in front of the block of units, and people could be heard coming and going inside.

After a while Roman became restless, stood up, and started pacing up and down the lawn. At this the listless policeman suddenly became alert. So Roman waved to him cheerfully and tried to convey the message that he was not edging towards the fence to make a rapid escape.

Standing on the lawn, he looked around. The other ground-floor units seemed to have similar small gardens. He stared upwards at the rest of the building towering overhead. Immediately above Jeff Ottway's backyard there was a vertical stack of pocket-handkerchief-sized balconies. Some of them held clothes-horses, loaded with clothes drying in the sun. Others were packed full of pot plants—small attempts to make gardens in the sky.

Roman walked as far as the paling fence, and then he noticed the policeman keeping him under surveillance becoming very restless indeed. So he decided that it would be more diplomatic to remain close to the Ottways' unit.

As he walked back down the gentle slope of lawn, Roman noticed a dark smear on the grass. It looked to him just like the dark smear of blood on the carpet inside the unit. He beckoned the policeman to come over.

'Look at this,' said Roman. 'Could this be blood?'

The young uniformed officer looked suspiciously at Roman, and then even more suspiciously at the dark stain on the grass.

'It could be. Come inside with me. We'll tell D.S. Marsh.'

Detective Marsh was in the lounge room supervising a scientific officer taking photographs of the body and the rest of the room. He was told about the possible bloodstain, and replied, 'In a minute.'

Roman returned outside to wait. He now began to examine his surroundings more closely. On the grass near his feet were a couple of cigarette butts. In his mind he began to reconstruct the crime.

'Alright, Roman,' Marsh interrupted his thoughts, 'what have you got for me?'

'The grass over here,' replied Roman, leading the way. 'See this dark stain? Could it be blood?'

Marsh looked at the stain for a moment without saying a word.

'And over there,' continued Roman, 'are some cigarette butts. Now I would reconstruct the crime like this: after talking to me Jeff Ottway still had an hour before he needed to go to work, so he stepped out here to smoke a cigarette or two. After all, it was a mild night. And it was here that he was attacked—where that stain is. Then his body was dragged inside and left where it is now.'

For a moment Detective Marsh's face flushed, and then, as though trying to restrain himself, he said carefully, 'Why? Why would Ottway's murderer bother to drag the body inside the unit? Answer me that!'

'Well, I can't say just yet . . .'

'No, of course you can't! This is exactly what I told you not to do, Mr Roman. Remember my orders: "Don't play amateur detective," I said. And what do I find? Within fifteen minutes, here you are trying to solve the case! Leave it to the experts. You are a witness. Possibly a suspect. Certainly *not* a detective! Do I make myself clear?'

'Yes. And I'm sorry if I offended you. I'm not trespassing on your territory. It's just that I noticed . . .'

'Just let me get on with my job, Mr Roman.'

And with that Marsh spun around and began to stomp back inside.

Roman took a deep breath. Clearly he had handled that badly. He glanced up at the uniformed officer near the sliding glass door. The young man looked embarrassed and turned away.

Well, decided Roman, if the police won't listen to me then I *will* conduct my own investigation. Hunting through his pockets, he found an old envelope containing an electricity bill. He stuffed the bill into a different pocket and began picking blades of the stained grass and packing them into the empty envelope. When he had a sizeable sample he carefully folded the envelope so that none of the grass could fall out, and put it into an inside pocket.

Roman sat down on one of the outdoor chairs. Given Marsh's annoyance, he suspected that he would be kept waiting. He was.

As the time dragged on, Roman began working through in his mind what he knew—looking for a

40

possible explanation for this ugly, violent end to a life.

Ottway had taken Roman's advice and confronted the person he had hurt. If Ottway's report was to be believed, he had confessed his deep guilt to that person, tried to communicate a sense of sympathy, and apologised. The response, again according to Ottway, had been hostile and abusive. The word he had used was 'vicious.'

Roman still did not know what offence Ottway was guilty of, nor what hurt he had inflicted. But imagine for a moment, Roman told himself, that it was a very serious injury. In fact, it must have been, to have haunted Ottway for so long. Alright, a deeply serious injury. And suppose further that the injured party had spent years burning up with anger—just as Ottway had spent years suffering from guilt.

These suppositions seemed reasonable enough. Could that anger, Roman asked himself, have grown to the point where it would motivate murder?

If the answer was 'yes,' then to find the murderer, it would be necessary to find the person Jeff Ottway had hurt all those years ago. That was certainly possible, Roman told himself: find the injured party and you find the murderer.

'Roman—you're wanted inside,' snapped McDermott from the doorway. Roman pushed his heavy frame out of the chair and stumped into the unit.

In the lounge room the body was being removed. Before the body bag was zipped up, Roman took another look at Jeff Ottway's face. It was deeply lined. It is said that in the repose of death people look younger. Ottway still looked anxious.

'How old was he?' asked Roman.

'None of your business,' snapped McDermott.

'From the birthdate on his driver's licence—thirty-six,' said Marsh, perhaps embarrassed by his partner's open hostility, or perhaps by his own earlier display of irritation.

'What time did you speak to Ottway, Mr Roman?' Marsh asked.

'About a quarter past midnight this morning.'

'And he told you that he was due at work in an hour's time?'

'That's right.'

'We've checked with his employer—he never turned up.'

'Did they try to find out where he was?' asked Roman.

'They rang here,' explained Marsh. 'The phone went unanswered. They didn't bother sending anyone around to check—they said they would only do that if he failed to turn up for several days in a row.'

'So, when did he die?' pursued Roman.

'Not long after you spoke to him—that's the preliminary guess of the GMO.'

'The GMO?'

'Government Medical Officer.'

'Ah, I see.'

During this exchange McDermott was becoming visibly irritated by his boss's willingness to exchange information with Roman.

'And just when did you leave your radio station this morning?' he interjected aggressively.

42

'Ten or fifteen minutes after the phone call from Ottway,' replied Roman.

'So about half past twelve, then?' continued McDermott.

'About that.'

'Any witnesses to that?'

'My producer, Andrew Gardner, and my panel operator, Peter Stanley. Ask them.'

'Oh, we intend to, Mr Roman, we fully intend to,' said McDermott. 'They work for you, I take it?'

'Yes, they do. But what difference does ... .'

'So they'd be prepared to lie for you then?'

'Oh, no, I wouldn't say that.'

'I would. So their evidence may not be enough to help you, Mr Roman.'

'I don't murder listeners,' barked Roman, his deep voice suddenly becoming cold and hard. Then he grinned and added, 'I need all the ratings I can get.'

'We have to check out every possibility,' Marsh intervened. 'It's just routine.'

'I understand,' Roman said. 'So what is your theory? Have you any idea of what happened here?'

'The most likely scenario,' replied Marsh, 'is a burglary gone wrong. Perhaps Ottway had turned off the lights preparatory to leaving for work and a would-be thief who was prowling around the building thought the occupants of the apartment were all asleep. For whatever reason, a burglar entered and Ottway was still here. The burglar—possibly someone with a drug habit, looking for ready cash—struck out, was alarmed to discover

43

he had killed Ottway, and fled without taking anything.'

'So nothing's missing?' asked Roman.

'That appears to be the case.'

'Why would a burglar break in here?'

'That's the easiest part to answer. It looks as though Ottway left the door onto the backyard unlocked by mistake. Any burglar prowling around the building looking for opportunities, trying all the doors and windows, would look on an unlocked door as a Christmas present.'

'I see,' muttered Roman thoughtfully.

'You're probably right about Ottway smoking on the lawn—and when he came in he forgot to lock the door behind him. My guess is that he then turned off the lights and started to leave for work. At about the same time as he was at the front door of this unit, the burglar was coming in through the garden door. What happened then? Impossible to say. Did Ottway realise that he had forgotten something—perhaps remembered the unlocked glass door—and come back into the unit? Or did he hear a noise and turn back to investigate? Whatever it was—the results were fatal.'

'But what about the problem he'd been talking to me about?' pursued Roman. 'This long-festering guilt, this person who had been hurt many years ago who was refusing to forgive him, and still felt a vicious anger towards him? Couldn't that be related to the death?'

'Possibly,' responded Marsh with a shrug of his shoulders, 'but less likely than the burglar scenario. We deal with a lot of deaths over the years, Mr Roman. The way I have described the incident is the most likely account of what happened.'

'What was the murder weapon?'

'None of this is any of your business, Roman!' interrupted an irritated McDermott.

'We like to keep people from the media happy, Don—if we possibly can,' said Marsh. 'And there's no reason why I can't answer your question, Mr Roman. Ottway was killed by a blow to the back of the head with a blunt instrument—a spanner, or tyre lever or something of that sort.'

'Have you found the weapon?'

'Not yet.'

'Ottway was struck from behind?'

'Yes. From behind, and by someone who was taller than him. A "high, arching blow" is the way the GMO described it. So the druggie we're looking for is tall—well over six feet. And probably male—it was a very heavy, savage blow. Some women could inflict a blow like that, but very few. So—male, and tall. And that's a good start.'

'And you don't think there's any possibility that my theory might have any merit at all?'

'What theory is that, Mr Roman?' said Marsh patiently, like a parent humouring a child.

Again Roman spelled out his ideas: the hurt inflicted long ago, the simmering guilt on one side and hatred on the other, the 'vicious' refusal to forgive—and all of this leading to a climax of violence.

'And can you give us any leads to follow up your theory, Mr Roman?' asked Marsh patiently.

'What sort of leads?'

'What was the incident—years ago—that sparked this off?'

'I'm afraid Jeff never revealed that.'

'And do you have any clues to the identity of the injured party?'

'Ah, none at all, I'm afraid—again, Jeff didn't say anything that would help there.'

'You see, Mr Roman—not only is your theory unlikely, it's also just about impossible to investigate.'

Marsh shrugged his shoulders helplessly, then turned back to his team to resume what he thought of as the 'real job'—the search for fingerprints or other physical clues that would stand up as evidence in court when they nailed their burglar.

For several minutes Roman watched them work, and then he asked, 'Am I needed any longer?'

'No—you're free to go,' Marsh said.

'For the time being,' McDermott added.

Roman shouldered his way past policemen and scientific equipment, out of the unit and back into the lobby of the building. For a moment he stood there, thinking about Jeff Ottway and his life in this block of home units with his young wife and daughter. A comfortable life no doubt, but cramped for a couple with a child.

Back on the street, standing in the warm, early afternoon sunshine, Roman noticed that beside the path leading to the front door was a steep drive-way running down to the underground car park in the basement of the building. As he watched, the steel roller door on the car park slowly opened and a car drove out. Acting on impulse, Roman walked quickly down the drive-way and into the car park before the door could slide closed again. If challenged, Roman would have said that he was not investigating—just trying to understand.

At this time of day, with most of the car spaces

46

empty, the car park was an echoing, concrete shell. Roman prowled around the area for a few minutes. Not really looking, or thinking, just trying to get the feel of life in this block.

He was interrupted by the low hum of a lift coming to a halt, followed by the hiss of lift doors opening. Roman walked in the direction of the sound. He saw an elderly couple emerge from the lift and walk towards their car. He watched them drive out, then he pressed the lift button and waited. A minute later it announced its arrival with a discreet bell.

Roman rode the lift back up to the lobby, where he surprised the policeman on the door by making his second exit in ten minutes. He walked back to where he had parked his own car, taking deep breaths to clear his head as he walked. He was not pleased to find a parking sticker on the windscreen of the Volvo, and wondered if being delayed by a murder investigation was an adequate defence against a parking violation.

He started the engine of the Volvo and turned the car not towards his home, but towards his radio station. Whatever else this murder was—it was a story, and Roman was still a radio man.

He parked the car in his marked space in the radio station basement, and took the lift up to the newsroom. Roman briefed Rob Raines, the duty editor, on the story, and then scripted and recorded a voice piece for the next news bulletin.

Next he called into the office of the station's program director, Tom Mutch.

'It's happened again, Tom,' said Roman as he walked into the office.

'What's happened again?'

'I've found a dead body—a murdered body.'

'Does the newsroom know?'

'I've just done a piece for them.'

'And they're first?'

'Yes, they'll break the story.'

'Good. We should also get you interviewed on the afternoon show—go and do that now. And while you're doing that, I'll call a few contacts in the press and spread the story. We might as well get some mileage out of this. Fill me in on the details.'

Roman handed over a copy of the script he had written for his news voicer. 'This'll give you the background.'

A few minutes later he was in studio one, sitting in the guest's chair and facing afternoon show host Dick Sherman across the console. The interview with Sherman lasted about ten minutes, and by the end of it Mutch had lined up press interviews with the *Herald* and the *Tele-Mirror*. Roman spoke to both of these journalists over the telephone from Mutch's office.

When he'd finished with the last of them he said, 'I'd like to take off for a while now, Tom—it's been a rough day, one way and another.'

'Yeah, of course, Mark. You go and have a break. Have you had any lunch?'

The question made Roman realise, with a start, that he had missed lunch entirely.

'Well, go and eat then,' said Mutch. 'Have a late lunch. Relax. And then come back here and have a chat to Brian Farrell so he can do follow-up pieces for drive-time and breakfast.' Brian Farrell was the station's police roundsman.

Roman left the radio station on foot, and walked

slowly to his favourite Italian restaurant, a few blocks away. It was late for lunch, but Giovanni always looked after him. After he ate a big bowl of minestrone, followed by tortellini, and gelato and a cappuccino, Roman was feeling very relaxed, not to say a little over-fed, and quite ready to face the rest of the day.

That night Roman's listeners wanted the full details. The older women were sympathetic, even motherly, towards him, and warned him of 'delayed shock' and other traumas that were about to strike him down.

As the evening wore on, and the studio got hotter, Roman removed his jacket. As he was taking it off he felt on odd bulge in the top pocket. Investigating, he came across his envelope of grass samples. In the midst of all that had happened, he had forgotten the grass he had collected.

He sat the envelope on the desk in front of him, and then decided to use the power of radio to do something about it.

As Peter Stanley waved him in after the commercial break, Roman began, 'I have in front of me an envelope filled with blades of grass. The grass has a dark stain on it—which I believe to be blood, although the police don't agree with me.'

He went on to explain how, and when, and where he had collected the sample.

'Now the reason I am explaining all this,' he continued, 'is because I would like to have this grass analysed. And I am wondering if there is an analytical chemist listening to the show tonight who might be able to help me out.'

The phone board went mad with offers of help. Most of them were useless; along the lines of 'I have an uncle in Brisbane who might be able to do it.' But it didn't take long—less than seven minutes—for a professional analytical chemist to ring in and offer to run some tests.

The result of this call was that the following morning at ten–thirty Roman drove into an industrial area at Rydalmere. After patient searching along a row of identical modern buildings he found the name he was looking for—Laboratory Consultancy Services. He parked in the spot marked 'visitor parking,' picked up his precious envelope of grass samples from the front passenger seat of the Volvo, and headed for the front door.

As he approached he read the large plastic sign above the front door that said: 'LCS—Providing a Complete Range of Chemical, Environmental and Microbiological Testing.' The glass double doors slid open and Roman found himself facing a reception desk staffed by two young women.

'Good morning, can I help?'

'I'm sure you can. My name is Mark Roman . . .'

'Oh, yes—it's Mark Roman,' she exclaimed before he could say any more. 'I listen every night, Mr Roman. I never miss your show.'

Roman thought ruefully that if everyone who told him they listened every night really did, his ratings would be double what they were.

'Your show is just terrific,' she continued.

'I'm pleased you like it,' said Roman, trying to turn on a pleasant smile. 'I'm here to see a Mr Ken Rodgers.'

'That'll be *Dr* Ken Rodgers. He's one of the partners. Take a seat, Mr Roman, and I'll let him know you're here.'

Roman took a seat on the plush lounge.

'He won't be a moment,' called out the receptionist.

'Thank you,' replied Roman, and smiled again.

He hunted through the magazines on the coffee table to see what sort of reading matter was provided for visitors. It turned out to consist entirely of back issues of a glossy magazine called *Industrial Chemist and Metallurgist*. Not exactly to Roman's taste.

But he didn't have much time to fill. Within two minutes a metallic door swung open and a man in a three-piece business suit emerged.

'Hello, Mark—I'm Ken Rodgers.'

Roman stood up and shook his hand. There must have been a look of disappointment on Roman's face, because Rodgers remarked, 'I'm sorry I'm not wearing a white coat or looking much like a mad scientist. I'm an administrator these days—I leave the benchwork to others. Let's have a look at your sample.'

Roman handed over the envelope, and once again ran over its history.

'Hmm. These stains certainly *could* be blood,' said Rodgers, holding several of the blades of grass in his fingertips, 'but only a lab test can tell for sure.'

'What exactly will you be able to tell me?' asked Roman.

'Two things. First, whether or not this is indeed human blood. And second—if it is—the blood group.'

'That should be enough to get the police to listen to my theory again,' muttered Roman.

'If—and I stress *if*—it does turn out to be blood,' cautioned Rodgers.

51

'Just find out what it is,' said Roman. 'I'm happy to abandon my theory if the evidence doesn't support it. How long will the test take?'

'Give us twenty-four hours. How can I contact you with the results?'

'Call my office at the radio station,' explained Roman, handing over his business card. 'That's the direct line. If I'm not there, the switch will pick up the call and you can leave a message.'

'You'll be hearing from us tomorrow then,' said Rodgers, and the two men shook hands again.

The drive back from Rydalmere gave Roman time to think about what he would do next. The police had not only dismissed his theory, they had told him it was almost impossible to investigate. That was like a red rag to a bull; Roman planned to demonstrate that it *could* be investigated. Besides which, the police had never spoken to Jeff Ottway, had not seen, as Roman had, the anguish in the man. Roman could not let go of the idea that being *unforgiven* lay at the heart of this violent death.

He drove to Chatswood, arriving in Cambridge Street shortly after midday. At the front door of the building he struck a snag. The police were gone, and the security system was operating. There was no way for him to get into the building unless someone inside let him in. Perhaps, thought Roman, he would get lucky, and get in as someone was leaving—as had happened the day before. But although he stood there waiting for five minutes the place was as quiet as the grave. No one came or went.

There was nothing for it, decided Roman, but to try one of the buttons. But what would he say?

The truth, Roman knew, was often the best approach. He picked one of the ground-floor buttons—marked with the name 'Neely'—and pressed it. After a wait of a minute a woman's voice said 'Hello?'

'Hello,' responded Roman, somewhat tamely. 'My name is Mark Roman—I discovered Jeff Ottway's body in his unit yesterday morning . . .'

'So I heard,' interrupted the voice crackling out of the grille. 'And I recognise your voice—come in, come in.'

A loud click told Roman that the front door was open. He pushed against it and it swung inwards. As he stepped inside the lobby one of the polished timber doors down the corridor swung open and a woman stepped out.

'Over here, Mark,' she called.

He walked in her direction. She looked to be in her sixties and was dressed in a flowing, pink house-dress, and nursing a small, white poodle.

'My name is Jayne Neely,' she introduced herself. 'And I'm a big fan of yours, Mark. And this is Rachel,' she added, turning to the poodle. 'Rachel, say hello to the nice man.'

The poodle looked at Roman with dark intelligent eyes as if to say 'Pay no attention to the baby-talk, I know what's really going on.'

Roman followed Jayne Neely, and the placid Rachel, into the Neely apartment. It was the mirror image of the one occupied by the Ottways—same design exactly, but turned around to face in the opposite direction.

'Tell me about yesterday, Mark. What happened? What did you find? How did you come to know young Mr Ottway?'

Roman decided that the best way to get information was to give it, so he told her everything she wanted to know, and patiently answered her questions.

After ten minutes of this her chatter came to an abrupt halt. 'But here I am, rattling on,' she said, 'and I haven't even offered you tea or coffee. Would you like a cup?'

'Only if you're having one yourself.'

'Oh, I am, I am. Which would you like—tea or coffee?'

'Coffee, please.'

'And how do you take it?' she called out over her shoulder as she waddled into the tiny kitchen.

'White with two sugars,' replied Roman.

While she was gone he took a look around the room. The decoration was all flowers and chintz. A tall bookcase beside the television set contained a collection of Barbara Cartland novels that was so large it probably deserved a place in the *Guinness Book of Records*.

'Here you are,' she said, 'white coffee with two sugars.'

Along with his coffee and her tea the silver tray that Jayne Neely placed on the coffee table was loaded with cream biscuits and chocolate biscuits. Roman sipped his coffee, and found that it had been made on milk, which he loathed.

'How's your coffee?' inquired Jayne, anxiously.

'Fine, thanks,' Roman lied. 'Now—I wonder if I might ask you a few questions?'

'Yes, of course, anything you wish, Mark dear.'

'Do you know the Ottways well?'

'Not very well. Just to speak to in passing. That sort of thing.'

'Did they seem like a happy couple?'

'As far as I could tell. Their little girl, Ellie, is very sweet. One of those quiet, well-behaved children. My Rachel took quite a fancy to little Eleanor, didn't you, pet?' Jayne Neely asked her dog, who raised her head a few centimetres off her front paws, decided nothing important was happening, and lowered it again.

'Were you home the night before last?'

'All of us were. My husband Bryce, and me, and little Rachel. We were all here.'

'Whatever happened to Jeff Ottway happened between midnight and one a.m.—did you hear anything between those hours, a disturbance of any kind?'

'I'm afraid not, Mark dear. I'd love to be able to help, but I'd just be telling fibs if I said I heard anything. I was sound asleep. I had taken my tablet, and I had my ear plugs in and my sleeping mask on. I didn't hear a thing.'

'You heard no disturbance of any kind?'

'On the weekend I heard an argument going on in one of the units—Dylan's I think. Or perhaps Miss Weston's. But nothing the night before last.'

'Can you tell me something about the occupants of the other units on the ground floor—in addition to yourselves and the Ottways?'

'Certainly. There are only four units on each floor, and the other two on this floor are occupied by Lorna Weston, a businesswoman of some sort, she's never here during the day; and Dylan Shumack, a handicapped young man—he sometimes plays music too loud and I have to thump on the wall to stop him. If I speak to him about

55

it, he's quite cheeky. I'm afraid I don't like him, Mark dear—handicap or no handicap.'

'Might your husband have heard something? The night before last, I mean?'

'He might have. Bryce is a lighter sleeper than me. You can ask him if you wish, he'll be back at five–thirty. Come back then, and ask him yourself.'

'I just might do that. Although the person I would really like to talk to is Jeff's wife.'

'Well, just go and knock on her door. Caitlin came home this morning.'

'Did she?'

'Yes. I presume the police must have contacted her yesterday afternoon, and she flew back from Wagga this morning. I saw her getting out of a taxi about an hour before you arrived.'

'Thank you, Jayne,' said Roman, rising to leave, 'you've been most helpful.'

'It's a pleasure, I'm sure. Oh, look—you haven't finished your coffee! Are you sure you don't want to finish it before you leave?'

'You mustn't spoil me, Jayne. And I do want to go and talk to Caitlin Ottway.'

'Yes, of course. Well, come back and see me again, won't you?'

'Certainly,' said Roman as he edged his way out of the door, 'yes, I certainly will.'

As soon the door of the Neely apartment closed behind him, Roman walked down the corridor to the Ottways' front door. He hesitated nervously, and then knocked.

The door was opened by a dark-haired, attractive young woman in her mid-twenties. Her eyes,

watery and red-rimmed, were a startling lavender
blue colour.

'Mrs Ottway?' said Roman.

She nodded.

'I'm Mark Roman.'

'Yes, I know who you are. Come in.'

CHAPTER 5

Roman followed Caitlin Ottway down the narrow
hallway and into the lounge/dining room. He
couldn't stop himself glancing at the spot where
Jeff Ottway's body had been twenty-four hours
earlier.

'I got to know your husband,' Roman explained,
as Caitlin waved him to a seat on the sofa, 'just a
few days before he . . . died.'

'He often talked about calling you, Mr Roman.
He admired you a lot.'

'Please call me Mark. And please accept my
condolences. I'm very sorry that I had to be the
one who found him.'

'Perhaps it's just as well,' she replied softly,
'otherwise it would have been Ellie and me who
found Jeff—when we came back from our holiday.'

'Is your daughter . . . ?'

'No, I left her with my parents. She's only three,
and it seemed the best thing to do.'

'Yes, I'm sure.'

'Did Jeff finally call you, Mr Roman . . . I'm
sorry, Mark?'

'Yes, he did.'

'About his nightmares?'

'No. What nightmares?'

'Jeff suffered from dreadful nightmares, Not

often, you understand, but when they came they were awful.'

'What were these nightmares about?'

'He never told me. But he woke up screaming, and dripping with sweat. If it wasn't the nightmares—what did he ring you about?'

'Guilt.'

'Guilt? Whose guilt? His? Mine? Somebody else's?'

'He said he was carrying a heavy burden of guilt—and had been for years.'

'Jeff? Feeling guilty?'

Caitlin Ottway looked completely puzzled, as if Roman was describing someone totally different from the man she had married. She ran her fingers through her short, black hair.

'What did Jeff have to feel guilty about?' she asked.

'He never told me,' explained Roman. 'I was hoping that he had told you.'

'I thought it was the nightmares that worried him . . . not guilt.'

'The two could be connected, of course,' murmured Roman. 'In fact, they almost certainly are.'

'Did he hint at what he felt guilty about?' asked Caitlin.

'Just that it was something that happened years ago, and resulted in someone else being hurt. How long have you known Jeff?'

'Not quite five years. We got married about seven months after we met. And Eleanor was born a year later.'

'So whatever was bothering him—causing the nightmares, and causing him to ring me about his

59

guilt problem—probably goes back to the time before you knew him?'

'I would say so. Perhaps it has something to do with his first marriage?'

'First marriage?'

'Didn't you know? Jeff got married very young. To a woman named Lesley—I don't know her last name. They were married for about five years. There weren't any children. Their marriage broke up quite some time before I met Jeff.'

'Did he ever talk about that break-up? Any hint of his feeling guilty about that?'

'Not really. When I asked him directly he said that he and Lesley just weren't compatible. But I think not having children may have had something to do with it.'

'Has he had any continuing contact with his first wife?'

'No. At least, not as far as I know. But I'm starting to wonder how well I knew Jeff after all. No, I'm pretty sure he didn't. There were no children, so there was no reason for continuing contact.'

'Of course,' muttered Roman. 'Which still leaves this puzzle of what he was so stressed about. Although I know that whoever it was he had hurt all those years ago, he spoke to again recently.'

'Really?'

'Yes. At my suggestion, I'm afraid. He wanted to know how to get rid of his burden of guilt, so I proposed apologising—getting it off his chest, and confessing his guilt to the person he had wronged. If that person had then been prepared to forgive him, the guilt would have been dealt with.'

'I see. And that's what Jeff has been talking to you about?'

'Yes.'

'All this is news to me.'

'Perhaps that's one of the reasons he called me about it now—while you were away. Perhaps he didn't want to risk his present happiness by raising old ghosts when you were around.'

'Perhaps. Look—I'm going to get myself a brandy, Mark. I think I need a drink. Can I get you something?'

'No, not just at the moment.'

'Coffee then?' asked Caitlin.

Roman remembered Jayne Neely's milky coffee and shuddered.

'No thanks,' he said.

When Caitlin returned from the drinks cabinet with a glass of brandy, she sat down facing Roman and asked, 'Could there be any connection between what Jeff was feeling guilty about and his death?'

'The police don't think so. In fact, they are sure it was a burglary gone wrong. I'm not so certain. Based on what Jeff told me, we're dealing with some pretty volatile emotions here—and they could have exploded in murder.'

'Jeff never appeared to be that . . . emotional . . . to me,' said Caitlin softly, once again running her fingers through her short, black hair. 'He was just an ordinary, easy-going, Aussie bloke. He was *my* bloke.'

When she said this, the tears welled up again and she buried her head in her hands and sobbed. Roman wanted to go over to her and put an arm around her and comfort her. But he was afraid this would be unwelcome. He was just an Aussie bloke—a typical, awkward Aussie bloke.

'I'm sorry about that,' whimpered Caitlin, dabbing her striking lavender blue eyes with a damp handkerchief.

'It's good for you to cry,' muttered Roman softly. 'It has to come out. That's what my mother used to say.'

'My mother too,' responded Caitlin, with a pale, little smile. 'Well, Mark—are you going to track down the dark secret in Jeff's past?'

'It might help find his murderer if I do. But would you rather that I didn't?'

'No. It's alright. I will go on loving Jeff, loving his memory, no matter what you find. And whatever the secret is, I just can't believe it's as horrible as all that.'

'I'm sure you're right,' murmured Roman comfortingly. 'But what I need is a starting point. Jeff's first wife might be a good place to start.'

'I'm afraid I can't help you there. I've no idea how to contact her. Although, perhaps she should be told that Jeff is dead. She would want to know.'

'What about his parents? Are they still alive?'

'Oh, yes. They still live in the family home.'

'Do you have the address?'

'Sure. Jeff and Eleanor and I visit them quite often.'

She turned around and opened a bureau drawer looking for pencil and paper. When she found these she wrote down the address and passed it over to Roman.

'That's them,' she said, 'Greg and Beryl Ottway. Oh, I've just had an awful thought!'

'What?'

'Has anyone told Greg and Beryl yet?'

'I'm sure the police will have been in touch with them.'

'Perhaps I should give them a ring?'

'I'm sure they'd appreciate that. And why don't you tell them that I'd like to call in for a chat some time soon.'

'Yes, I'll tell them you're coming.'

Roman stood up to leave, and Caitlin walked to the door ahead of him.

'I'm glad you called in, Mark. You're just as nice as you sound on the radio.'

'Well,' murmured Roman, feeling embarrassed, 'if there's anything I can do to help—you get in touch. Promise?'

'I promise. And thanks again.'

Roman walked slowly and thoughtfully across the lobby. He was almost at the front door when he stopped in his tracks. While he was here, inside the building, he decided, he should keep on investigating.

He turned aside and looked at the doors of the units he had not yet visited. One belonged to a disabled man—no friend of Jayne Neely's—and the other to a businesswoman named Weston. Roman checked his watch—half past four. The businesswoman was unlikely to be home, but the young man might be there.

There were no names marked on the doors, so Roman could only take a chance on which was which. The first door he tried produced no results despite prolonged knocking. Right, thought Roman, that must be Ms Weston's unit. He turned his attention to the other door. And here his knocking produced a response almost at once.

'I'm coming,' called out a voice from within. But it was a minute or two before the door actually opened.

Roman found himself facing a young man, an extremely fat young man, in a wheelchair.

'Hi,' he said in his warm radio voice, 'I'm Mark Roman.'

'G'day, Mark,' chirped the young man, 'I'm Dylan Shumack—and I'm a fan. What can I do for you?'

'I'd like to ask you some questions about Jeff Ottway.'

'The guy who died?'

'That's right.'

'Sure. Come in.'

He backed his wheelchair up the narrow hall, and then spun it deftly around into the lounge/dining room. The same room pattern as in the Ottways' unit was repeated here.

'Take a seat, Mark. I know that you found the body.'

'That's right. How did you know?'

'I listened to your show last night. And because I live in the units I knew more than all the other listeners just what you were talking about. How can I help? Am I a witness?'

'Possibly. Have the police already questioned you?'

'Briefly. But they didn't seem interested in anything I said.'

'Oh? What did you tell them?'

'I told them I'd seen a man hanging around the Ottways' unit. He didn't seem to be going anywhere—just hanging around. Maybe he was waiting for someone, but he looked suspicious to me.'

'Really! Now that is interesting. Can you describe the man?'

'I never saw his face, but he had red hair, and every time I saw him he was wearing a leather jacket—like a motorbike jacket.'

'What about his build? Can you describe that?'

'Tall and thin. And that's about all—tall and thin, with red hair and a leather jacket.'

'And the police weren't interested in this information?'

'Didn't seem to be. The bloke who talked to me was a Detective McDermott, and everything I said he challenged.'

'Don't worry,' reassured Roman, 'I've had my run-ins with McDermott as well. That's just his manner. If you told him exactly what you've just told me, I assure you the police are taking it very seriously.'

'Oh? Well, good then. What about you? How are you involved, Mark?'

'I found the body.'

'But before that,' persisted Shumack, 'how did you get involved with Ottway?'

'He rang my show—wanted some advice. We met last Saturday at an art show at Chatswood Civic Centre and then he rang again, and he was sounding pretty desperate, so I agreed to come here to his place to talk to him.'

'So you didn't really know him well at all?'

'No, not really.'

'Oh. Look—would you like a Coke?'

'That'd be nice. Yes please.'

'Hang on here, Mark—I'll get it for you.'

The tubby young man spun his wheelchair around with precise skill and headed for the kitchen. Roman could see that the kitchen cupboards had been especially lowered, and there were railings on the walls at certain places. The other distinctive feature of the unit was the mess! There were videos, CDs, comic books and paperback books, piled on every available surface and scattered across the floor. It occurred to Roman that the mess on the floor was not a good idea for a person who needed a wheelchair!

Dylan Shumack soon came speeding back, two cans of Coke in his lap. He threw one to Roman, and pulled the top off the other.

Roman took a sip of the cold liquid, and then asked, 'What's unit-living like for someone in a wheelchair?'

'In this unit it's okay. That's why I'm here. The front path is flat, and there's a ramp at the front door. This building is wheelchair-friendly. But the big thing is the elevator—without that I couldn't get from the car park up to here.'

'Oh, you drive, do you?'

'Sure do. I'm a demon on the road, Mark,' said Shumack with a laugh.

'I'll believe you,' commented Roman, 'I've seen what you do with that thing in this confined space. So, you have a specially equipped car, I take it?'

'That's right. All hand controls—hand throttle, and so on.'

'What about getting in and out of the car? Or maybe I shouldn't be asking you these personal questions?'

'No—I don't mind. I've got a machine fitted to the roof-rack of the car—a sort of lift. It helps me in and out of the car, and then stores the folded-up wheelchair on the roof-rack.'

'Very clever. How do you get on with the other people in the units?'

'Most of them are okay. Except for that old Neely bat next-door. She's always whingeing. One of these days I'm going to run right over that little dog of hers. That'll teach her!' said Shumack with a gleeful cackle.

Roman took another pull on his Coke and then asked, 'Ottway was killed the night before last. Some time between midnight and one a.m., the police think. Did you hear anything between those hours?'

'Not a thing, Mark old buddy. I have a lot of difficulty sleeping—because this chair stops me getting enough exercise or something. So my doc gives me little white pills to zonk me out at night. I'd taken one the night before last and I wouldn't have heard an atom bomb go off.'

'How long have you been in these units?'

'Not long. Three or four months. About that.'

'And coming back to this bloke you saw—tall, thin, red-haired, leather jacket.'

'What about him?'

'When did you see him?'

'First time—two weeks ago. Last time—on Sunday.'

'That's very interesting, Dylan,' muttered Roman. 'Thank you for that.'

Roman finished his Coke and then stood up.

'Well, I should get going—I've taken up enough of your time.'

'The one thing I've got heaps of, Mark old buddy, is time—heaps of time.'

'I still have to get going.'

'Hey, listen—I wanted to say, I often listen to

67

your show, but I've never rung in. I'd like to. Is it okay with you if I ring in some night—just to be on the air?'

'Sure. You're more than welcome.'

'And why don't you drop in again some time—tell me what it's like hosting a radio talk-back show. I'd like to know about that.'

'Okay—I will.'

Roman made his farewells and let himself out of Dylan Shumack's unit.

As he stepped into the corridor he saw a woman putting her key into the door of the unit opposite.

'Excuse me,' said Roman, 'would you be Ms Weston?'

'I'm Lorna Weston,' she replied, in a rather haughty tone. 'And who might you be?'

'I'm Mark Roman—I discovered the body of Jeff Ottway in his unit yesterday morning.'

'Yes, I read about it in the newspaper. Well?'

'I was wondering if you'd answer a few questions?'

'I will not be part of any publicity stunt!'

'This is not a publicity stunt,' urged Roman in his most persuasive voice. 'This is something I have to do. I feel that I let Jeff Ottway down in the last days of his life—and I'm not going to let him down in his death.'

'Very well,' she said reluctantly, 'you can come in for five minutes. But only five minutes. I have to get changed—I'm going out tonight.'

Roman followed Lorna Weston into the unit. She had very closely cropped blonde hair and was power-dressed in a smart suit. He guessed she was in her mid-thirties.

Once again, the layout of the unit aped its

68

fellows, but the difference in this one was the quality of the furnishings—clearly a lot of money had been spent.

'Take a seat, Roman,' Lorna Weston said. 'Would you like a drink?'

'Not just at the moment,' Roman replied as he sank his heavy frame into a leather-covered armchair.

She poured two fingers of Jack Daniels into a whisky glass, and sat down opposite him. As she relaxed into the comfort of the sofa she kicked off her shoes and sighed deeply.

'Ah, that's better. Now—ask your questions, Mr Roman, you only have five minutes.'

'Jeff Ottway died the night before last between midnight and one a.m. Did you hear any suspicious noises?'

'It all depends on what you call suspicious, doesn't it?'

'Did you hear anything at all?'

'I don't think I heard the murderer, if that's what you mean. There's always some movement in a building as big as this, and that's what I heard.'

'Could you be more specific.'

'Alright—I heard the front door open and close several times. This is the closest unit to the entrance, and when it's quiet at night I always hear the front door open and close.'

'Anything else?'

'I heard a car pull into our driveway at one stage. The lift operated a couple of times. The usual sorts of noises one hears at night in a building of this sort.'

'And those sounds you've just listed—you heard all those between midnight and one a.m.?'

'That was the time you specified, wasn't it?'

'How well do you know the Ottways?'

'They're what I call "weather people."'

'Which means . . . what, exactly?'

'It means that all I have ever talked to them about is the weather: "Nice day, isn't it?" and "Unseasonably hot, wouldn't you say?"—that sort of thing.'

'I see. Did you like them?'

'What's to dislike? They seemed pleasant enough. She struck me as an intelligent young woman wasting her life married to a tradesman. Mind you, she's besotted with that child of theirs, and small children are enough to turn the brain into porridge!'

'Did they strike you as being happily married?'

'They didn't strike me at all, Mr Roman. Whether they were deliriously happy or wallowing in misery is not a question I ever concerned myself with.'

'One other question . . .'

'No other question,' Lorna Weston interrupted. 'You've had your five minutes, and I have to get changed and go out. Thank you for your company, Mr Roman—you know where the door is.'

On his way out he said over his shoulder, 'Do you mind if I call back another day—should some more questions occur to me?'

'You can try your luck if you wish, Mr Roman. I'm a big girl, I can say "no" if you're annoying me.'

Back in the lobby of the building Roman checked his watch: it was just after five–thirty and that meant that Jayne Neely's husband might be home from work. Might as well polish off the last interview while I'm here, he thought, and he knocked on the door of the unit.

It was Jayne who opened the door.

'Mark!' she gushed, 'how lovely to see you again! Do come in.'

As she threw the door open wide, Roman's nostrils were assailed by the smell of food cooking—presumably the Neelys' evening meal. It was not an appetising smell, composed, as it was, of equal parts of cabbage and fish.

'I've just called to see if your husband is in,' explained Roman.

'Yes, Bryce is home,' responded Jayne. 'He got in five minutes ago.'

Roman followed his hostess, a shimmering vision in pink, into the lounge/dining room. There he met Bryce: a pale, grey man, dressed in an old cardigan and house slippers. After the introductions, and more offers of tea and coffee, which Roman politely declined, he and Bryce sat down opposite each other.

'I take it your wife has told you what this is about, Mr Neely?'

'Yes, she has. Couldn't talk of anything else, ever since I got home.'

'Sorry about that,' murmured Roman quietly, so that Mrs Neely, pottering about in the kitchen, couldn't hear.

'Not your fault, old man,' snorted Bryce. 'She gets obsessed with radio talk-back stars and TV soap operas. She doesn't have enough to occupy her mind—that's the trouble.'

'The night before last,' continued Roman, 'is the time I'm concerned about.'

'That's when poor young Jeff copped it, eh?'

71

'Precisely. Some time between midnight and one a.m.: did you hear anything? Your wife says you're a lighter sleeper than her.'

'Quite right too. But I don't think I heard the murder being committed, if that's what you're after.'

'But did you hear anything—anything at all?'

'Nothing sinister, old man, nothing sinister at all. Just the usual noises one hears in a building of this size at that time of night.'

'Such as?'

'Just the occasional person moving about, that's all. Like I say—nothing sinister. Sorry I can't be more help.'

At that point Jayne re-appeared from the kitchen, bubbling with energy.

'Would you like to stay to dinner, Mark? We've plenty of food, it would be no stretch I assure you.'

'That's a very kind offer, Jayne,' said Roman, rising to his feet, 'but I really have to get to the station and do some prep for tonight's show.'

'Oh, yes, of course. How foolish of me.'

Roman was moving quickly towards the door during these remarks, and so it was with his hand on the door knob that he said, 'Thank you again for your hospitality. And for your help. Both of you.'

'A pleasure, old chap,' said Bryce.

'Call again. Any time,' said Jayne.

And with those words ringing in his ears Roman made his escape.

That night on the show Roman's listeners kept wanting to come back to the subject of forgiveness. Person after person had their own list of actions that they could never forgive. Some talked about the war between the Serbs and the Bosnians, others about the killings in Rwanda, and others about more personal incidents.

'It has actually happened to me,' said Denise of Cronulla.

'What's happened?' Roman rumbled into the microphone, in his distinctive deep voice.

'The unforgivable has been done to me.'

'What was it exactly?'

'I'm not sure I want to say.'

'Well, don't name names, and be a bit vague if you want to, but you must give us some idea, if we are to understand what you're saying.'

'Very well then. I might as well say it. It was over a will.'

'Yes? Go on.'

'After Mum died, my elder sister went to the house and just scooped up everything she felt like taking. Before the body was even cold. That was bad enough to begin with. Later on she denied that she had done it, but the neighbours saw her and they told me.'

'But I take it there was more?'

'There certainly was, Mark. When the will was read, it turned out that Mum had left the house to me, and just a few small things to Eileen. Well, that's the way it should be because I was the one who looked after Mum when she was old, not Eileen. Anyway, Eileen split up the family by going to law over it. She dragged me and my hubby through the courts for years. She lost, but she cost us a lot of money in legal fees. In fact, she cost us most of what we got out of the house. Looking back on it now, we might as well have just given her the house in the first place. Except

73

I could never have done that, because I couldn't stand to see her gloat.'

'Or maybe just divided the value of the house with her when you sold it—so that she had no reason to go to court?'

'But Mum left it to *me*! Not to Eileen. It would have been going against Mum's wishes to share it with Eileen.'

'But would your Mum have wanted her family to be split, the way you say it is now?'

'No, of course not. But that's Eileen's fault, not mine.'

'Look,' said Roman, taking a deep breath and trying to be patient, 'when someone deceives you, or hurts you, or frightens you—which is what facing a law court does, it frightens people—your body gears up to fight or run away. In extreme cases, people can suffer heart attacks or strokes as a result of cruel words or horrible actions.'

'That's right, Mark!' shrieked the caller. 'What Eileen did nearly broke my health.'

'All the more reason for reconciling and forgiving.'

'Eh?'

'Feeling angry when you have been hurt by someone is not wrong. It is a normal reaction and the sign of a healthy personality. But the hurt and the anger must not be ignored. They must be dealt with or else they will fester inside and affect *your* emotional health, Denise—not Eileen's.'

'But *she's* the one who's done it!'

'Yes, I know. But you can still be the one who ends it—if you want to be.'

'What you do mean?'

'Ideally, talking things over, telling the other

party—quietly and gently—that you have been hurt by them, will be followed by reconciliation with the person who caused the hurt.'

'You only say that because you don't know Eileen!'

'Well, suppose you refuse to talk it over. In that case, the anger you felt at the beginning will not go away. Instead, it settles down into a long-term resentment. Every time you think about it, you smoulder inside. It worms its way into your personality and begins to infect other relationships.'

'But with someone like Eileen . . .' wailed the caller.

'Hear me out,' insisted Roman. 'Every doctor knows patients whose chronic conditions are made worse by resentment. Initial anger may be healthy, but long-term unhealed anger may be very dangerous indeed. For your own good, Denise, you need to learn how to forgive.'

'But you don't understand! Eileen is the one who did all this!'

'Let me put this challenge to you, Denise: if Eileen came up to you tomorrow and said, "I'm sorry about what I did, please forgive me"—would you forgive?'

'She won't. Eileen's not like that.'

'I know, I know. But can't you use your imagination? Just pretend she said that to you—would you forgive her?'

'You're not listening to me, Mark,' screeched Denise of Cronulla. 'Eileen will *never* apologise.'

'I give up,' muttered Roman into the mic. 'Maybe there's something wrong with *me*, if I can't help Denise to understand. Thanks for your call, Denise—good night.'

75

'Good night, Mark.'

'Nick from Hornsby is next. Evening Nick.'

'Evening, Mark. Boy you were patient with that woman. I don't know what's wrong with her.'

'I'm afraid I do,' commented Roman sadly. 'Eaten up with resentment—that's the problem. The worm of resentment is eating out her heart.'

'And her mind, by the sound of it,' said Nick.

'Now that's being a little unfair,' chuckled Roman, 'but I can't say you're wrong.'

All through his conversation with Denise, Roman had been thinking of the murderer of Jeff Ottway. Was the murderer that sort of person? Someone whose heart, and conscience, and moral sense, had been eaten away by the worm of resentment? Is that what led to the killing in the early hours of Tuesday morning? Was it a refusal to forgive that caused more damage than the original hurt?

Coming out of the ten–thirty news headlines, Roman referred back to the call from Denise.

'I keep thinking about what she was saying,' he told his listeners, 'and the thing that strikes me is this: for us to forgive, perhaps we need first to taste forgiveness ourselves. Maybe that's the key. When we experience generous, overwhelming forgiveness, *then* we have the model and the inner strength to forgive others. And, of course, we can only experience that sort of forgiveness from the hand of God.'

Roman took a sip from his mug of coffee and then glanced at the computer screen.

'Ken of Rydalmere,' he read, 'is next. Evening, Ken.'

'Evening, Mark. It's me—your friendly, neighbourhood analytical chemist.'

'Ah, Ken! I didn't connect the name when I saw it on the screen.'

'I'm calling tonight to tell you that we finished those tests more quickly than I'd predicted.'

'And you have the results?'

'I do indeed. Would you like me to give them to you on the air?'

'Why not? I'll look like an idiot if it's not blood, but I've looked like an idiot before—so you might as well go for it.'

'Well, the good news, Mark, is that you are not an idiot—the staining is definitely human blood.'

'What a relief! Anything more?'

'Yes, I can give you the blood group.'

'Which is?'

'The blood on the grass samples belongs to type O.'

'And does that tell us anything?'

'Unfortunately, type O is the most common blood group in the world, so it might not be useful. On the other hand, if the victim *was* type O . . . well, you would have to say it was suggestive, wouldn't you?'

'You certainly would!' agreed Roman with glee. 'Now can you give me an official written report of your analysis?'

'Certainly. I'll have it faxed to your radio station tomorrow—how would that be?'

'Excellent. And I'll contact the police tomorrow to see if they're interested in the results. Ken, thanks for all your help.'

'My pleasure, Mark. Any time.'

At nine–thirty the next morning Roman was sitting in his apartment, dialling the number of the Chatswood Police Station.

'Chatswood Police.'

'Detective branch, please.'

'Putting you through.'

There was a pause, and a click, and then another voice answered, 'Chatswood detectives, Marsh speaking.'

'Just the man I wanted. It's Mark Roman here.'

'I knew that the moment you opened your mouth, Mr Roman. What can I do for you?'

'I had the stain on the grass outside Jeff Ottway's unit checked by an analytical chemist. It was human blood.'

'I see,' responded Marsh in a hushed tone that could have indicated either interest or anger. 'And did you have it typed?'

'Yes. Type O.'

'The most common in the world,' commented Marsh.

'But was Jeff Ottway's blood group type O?' persisted Roman.

There was a long pause before the detective answered.

'Yes, it was, Mr Roman,' he said at last, 'so you can savour your little moment of triumph. But, as I said, type O is the most common, and the stain you found probably means no more than that the lawn mower man cut himself last time he was there. From now on, please leave the detecting to the professionals.'

CHAPTER 6

Roman looked at the phone for a long time after he had hung up. He didn't feel angry with Marsh, and he understood how irritating it must be to have an amateur playing on your turf. Roman himself felt the same way about politicians, and ex-politicians, and politicians' wives, and ex-politicians' ex-wives who tried their hand at hosting radio talk-back shows.

But although Roman was sympathetic, he wasn't going to stop his investigation.

Besides, he told himself, it wasn't really an investigation. He and the police had quite different goals in mind. For the police, what mattered was getting someone in the dock with enough evidence to convict. For Roman, what mattered was *understanding* why people behaved the way they did, and why a life ended in violent death.

Roman walked over to the window of his apartment that looked down on Milson Park. Sydney's indian summer had disappeared overnight. The sunlight looked pale and watery, and the wind blowing in off Careening Cove and tossing the palm trees in the park looked decidedly chilly.

For a while he paced restlessly up and down the narrow space in his apartment wondering what he could do next to decipher the puzzle of Jeff Ottway's past. Then he decided.

Roman drove back to Cambridge Street, Chatswood, and pressed the button marked 'Neely'.

'Hello?'

'It's me again, Jayne.'

'Come in, Mark. I was half-expecting you to come back today.'

The front door clicked and Roman pushed it open. Jayne was waiting at the open door to her unit as he crossed the lobby. She was wearing another floating house-dress—in striking egg-shell blue today.

'Come in and have a cup of coffee, Mark,' she said cheerily.

Roman shuddered inwardly.

'Later,' he replied. 'For the moment I was wondering if you know any of the occupants of the first-floor units.'

'The first floor?'

'Yes. I thought one of them might have heard something on the night Jeff Ottway died. Particularly if I'm correct about his being killed out on the lawn. There's no point trying any of the higher units, but on the first floor someone may have heard something.'

'Yes, yes, I can see that,' Jayne said earnestly. 'As it happens, I do know two of the people on the first floor. Well, three, actually. There's Meg and Jason Palmer. Lovely young couple. They have the end unit on the first floor—right above the Ottways'. And then there's Miles Temperton. Quite a gentleman, he is. Very nice manners. He has the unit over this one.'

'I'll pop up and have a chat to them,' Roman said. 'Thanks for your help, Jayne.'

'You won't find the Palmers there, I'm afraid, Mark dear.'

'They both work, do they?'

'On holidays—that's where they are. Due back this week, I think. But they're not back yet. I'm sure I would have seen them if they were.'

'Well, I'll try Miles Temperton anyway.'

'And come back and tell me how you get on, Mark dear. I'll have some coffee on the stove ready for you.'

Jayne Neely bobbed back inside her unit, and Roman pressed the button to summon the lift. It was slow in arriving and Roman felt guilty about not taking the stairs. For only one floor, taking the lift seemed a trifle lazy. But, like a lot of heavy, flat-footed men, Roman would never walk when he could ride.

The lift arrived at last and quietly hummed him up to the first floor.

Once there he had to get his bearings and work out which unit would be directly above the Neelys'. When he had done this, he knocked at the door. The response was slow in coming, and eventually he heard shuffling footsteps and the door opened.

'Yes?' Before him was a florid-faced man in his seventies, with a stern expression and an erect, military bearing.

'Mr Miles Temperton?'

'Major Temperton, to be absolutely correct. What can I do for you?'

'My name is Mark Roman, and Jayne Neely suggested that you might be able to help me.'

'In what way?'

'I'm the person who discovered the body of Jeff

81

Ottway on Tuesday morning. And I'm trying to find out something about his background, and why he was killed.'

'You'd better come in then.'

Roman closed the door behind him as he followed Temperton—who walked with a pronounced limp—into another of the standard-plan apartments.

'I've just put the kettle on,' the old man said. 'Will you join me for a cup of Earl Grey?'

'I'd be delighted.'

'Take a seat then while I make up a pot. Don't believe in tea bags. Horrid things. Not real tea.'

Roman lowered his heavy frame into an overstuffed armchair, and looked around the room. It was cluttered with black-and-white photographs—mainly family pictures or groups of young men in uniform.

'Lemon or milk?' asked Temperton, as he shuffled in from the kitchen carrying a tray.

'How very civilized,' remarked Roman. 'Lemon, please.'

The major used silver tongs to drop a thin slice of lemon into Roman's tea, and then held up a sugar bowl.

'One lump or two?'

'Two please.'

The same tongs were used for the sugar cubes. Roman slowly stirred his tea while Temperton poured his own.

'Now,' said the major, once he was leaning back in his armchair, nursing his fine china tea cup, 'what do you imagine I might be able to tell you?'

'For a start, I was wondering if you heard anything on the night of the murder.'

'Unlikely. I'm afraid my ears aren't as sharp as they used to be. When was this exactly?'

'Monday night. Or, rather, the start of Tuesday morning. Between midnight and one a.m.'

'As it happens, I think I was awake then. One of my bad nights.'

'Bad nights?'

'Gout. A touch unpleasant occasionally.'

Roman understood this to mean that it was sometimes excruciatingly painful.

'Monday night–Tuesday morning?'

'That's right,' said Temperton, 'I was awake then.'

'And did you hear anything?'

'I heard some noises. I had the window open—it was such a mild night. But only very ordinary noises, I'm afraid. Nothing that sounded like murder being done.'

'Jeff Ottway was killed by a single blow to the back of the head. So it may not have sounded very much like murder. What noises did you hear then?'

'Let's see. I'll try to remember precisely. Midnight to one a.m., you say?'

'That's right.'

'I remember hearing the roller door downstairs operate. I thought to myself that someone was coming home very late for a weeknight.'

'Or possibly going out very late?'

'No, they were coming in, definitely. If they'd been going out I'd have heard the car engine as they accelerated up the ramp from the basement.'

'Right. What else?'

'The lift went past this floor once or twice. I heard a car door slam. Or possibly a car boot. I can't be sure which.'

'I thought you said your hearing wasn't very good?'

'Not as good as it once was.'

'It's still not too bad. Now, these noises you heard—most of them were from outside?'

'That's right. Through my open window. These units are quite well soundproofed—not totally, of course, but quite well. So with the door closed and the window open I could hear sounds from outside better than I could hear sounds from inside the building.'

'Did you ever meet the Ottways?'

'Only once. At a dinner party at the Neelys'.'

'What impression did you form?'

'Not a very strong one. Nice young couple. That's about it. I was impressed by their kid. A polite, well-behaved child.'

'And there's nothing else you can tell me?'

'I can't think of anything, I'm afraid, Mr Roman.'

'Well, thank you for the tea, Major . . .'

'Call me Miles—most people around here do.'

'Thank you for the tea, Miles—it was delicious.'

Roman rose from his seat and waited, giving Temperton time to show him to the door, walking ahead of him with his stiff-legged gait.

'One last thing,' Roman said, pausing on the threshold, 'I know the Palmers live in the end unit on this floor—who occupies the other two?'

'They are both occupied by single people. April Myers lives next door to me and young Morgan Simmonds lives across the way—he's a merchant banker, I think.'

'Well, thank you again for your time, Miles,' said Roman shaking the old man's hand. Once the door had closed behind him, Roman knocked at each of the other units. He got no response at either. Apparently the Palmers were still on holiday, Morgan Simmonds was at work, and April Myers was out doing whatever she was doing.

As Roman turned to leave he heard the lift hum, and the lift doors hiss open. Out stepped a man in his late twenties carrying a suitcase and pushing a wheelchair. In the wheelchair was an extraordinarily pretty young woman, with honey blonde hair and green eyes. Both were tanned and wearing casual clothes. This had to be the Palmers returning from their holiday.

'Excuse me,' said Roman.

The couple stopped in their tracks and looked at him without saying anything.

'You wouldn't be the Palmers by any chance, would you?'

'Yes, we are,' replied the young man, 'Jason and Meg Palmer. And you are . . . ?'

'My name is Mark Roman . . .'

'From the radio?' exclaimed Meg. 'Yes! Of course you are! I'd know that voice anywhere. We haven't won a prize, have we?'

'I'm afraid not.'

'Then what can we do for you?' Jason asked.

'While you've been away there's been a tragedy in the building.'

'A tragedy? What sort of tragedy?' asked Meg, suddenly sobered.

'A death, I'm afraid.'

'Who?'

'Jeff Ottway.'

'Oh, no!' gasped Meg, going pale underneath her tan.

'Poor Caitlin,' murmured Jason.

'And poor little Eleanor,' added Meg. 'How did he die?'

'He was murdered.'

'Murdered?' Jason repeated. 'I don't understand. Look—rather than stand here, you'd better come inside and tell us all about it.'

'I'll take Mr Roman in, you go and get the other cases, sweetheart,' suggested Meg.

Jason disappeared back into the lift, while Meg led the way to her front door, spinning her wheels with the same speed and precision Roman had seen earlier in Dylan Shumack. Roman carried the suitcase Jason had set down by the lift. Meg unlocked the door and led the way into her apartment.

'Where have you been on your holiday?' asked Roman, making conversation until Jason returned.

'Club Med, Vanuatu—it was fabulous. But it rather takes the gloss off the holiday to come home to news like this.'

'I'm sorry to spoil it for you.'

Just then Jason arrived, staggering under the weight of two large suitcases. He dropped these in the hall next to the one Roman had set down, took a seat by Meg and looked questioningly at Roman.

'I was the one who found the body. Jeff had been killed by a blow to the back of the head.'

'When was this?' Jason asked.

'I found him on Tuesday morning. He'd been killed the night before—not long after midnight.'

'It's so sad,' whispered Meg, her green eyes becoming moist.

'Who on earth would want to kill Jeff?' muttered Jason, a look of utter bewilderment on his face.

'The police think it was a burglar who was disturbed by Jeff. But I'm not so sure.'

'So—what do you think?' Meg asked.

'Jeff had rung me on my show a couple of times, and off the air as well, and met me, to talk about a problem he had—a feeling of guilt about something that went back quite a few years.'

'Guilt? Jeff? About what?'

'I never found out. But I have a feeling that if I can, I'll also find out who killed him.'

Roman explained his theory to them—the bitterness and lack of forgiveness that remained vicious, even after years, and that ended in murder.

'Let me get this straight,' said Jason. 'You're saying that after Jeff made contact with this person—whoever it is—last weekend and was rebuffed, this same person found Jeff smoking a cigarette on the lawn, just after midnight on Monday, and killed him by bashing him over the head with a tyre lever?'

'Something like that, yes.'

'It seems so extraordinary,' murmured Meg.

'So how well did you two know the Ottways?' Roman asked.

'Reasonably well, I suppose,' replied Jason.

'Probably better than anyone else in this building,' added Meg, 'It's an age thing. We were both young couples. A lot of the other people, at least on these lower floors, are either older or single.'

'Did Jeff ever say anything to you—or even hint—about what this source of his guilt might be?'

'Not a word to us. What about Caitlin? Have you spoken to her?'

'She was as surprised as you two. But it fits in

with the nightmares Jeff used to have from time to time.'

'Nightmares? This is something else I haven't heard about,' Jason said.

'I knew,' said his wife. 'Caitlin told me about the nightmares a few months ago. She asked me not to mention it to anyone. It was girl talk. You know.'

'What about his first wife? Could it have anything to do with her?'

'I doubt it. Jeff hardly ever mentioned her. What's her name, Jason? Is it Leigh?'

'No . . . it's . . .'

'Lesley,' interrupted Roman.

'That's right! Lesley, that's it.'

'Did she ever visit? Did Jeff have any contact with her?'

'Oh, no. I'm certain not,' muttered Meg, shocked. 'She was in the past. Over and done with. Do you think this past guilt had something to do with her?'

'It's a possibility,' shrugged Roman. 'What about other people in the block? Did they have much to do with the Ottways?'

'Not really. People are nice here, but a bit distant,' explained Jason, 'if you know what I mean.'

'I think I do. Well, look—you've been more than helpful, but I guess you two want to unpack. I should let you get on with it.'

As he spoke, Roman stood up and moved towards the door.

'Feel free to come back any time you want. We'd like to give you any help we can,' said Meg, spinning her wheels around to follow him. As she did so, Roman noticed the black, rubber tyre marks on the skirting boards—unavoidable, he supposed, when there was a wheelchair in the apartment.

'Do you mind if I ask you a question, Meg?'

'Ask anything you like, Mark.'

'How long have you been in the wheelchair?'

'Twelve years now—since I was thirteen. And to save you asking—it was a car accident that did it.'

'I'm sorry to hear that.'

'Don't be. Us wheelies don't want anyone's sympathy. Life can be just as rich and satisfying for us as it can be for any of you leggies.'

'Looking at you, Meg, I can believe that,' Roman remarked. 'But not all paraplegics have your attitude.'

'I know, I know. I spend a lot of my time trying to get the message through to the "poor me" types and the depressives. Like Dylan downstairs, for instance.'

'Is he a depressive?'

'He doesn't have to work—he lives off the interest from a big insurance pay-out. But the result is that he doesn't get involved with anyone else. He doesn't socialise. Between you and me, Mark, I'm trying to bring him out of himself a bit. We had him keep an eye on our unit while we were away, just to give him a sense of responsibility. And I know some girls in wheelchairs about Dylan's age who would like to meet him. But so far I haven't succeeded in dragging him out to any of the social functions.'

'But she will,' added Jason. 'Once she's made up her mind to do something, there's no stopping Meg. If she's decided to get young Dylan matched up, she'll do it!'

Roman left the building cheered by the positive

attitude and youthful energy of the Palmers. Outside, a chilly wind was blowing papers down Cambridge Street, and gathering grey clouds threatened rain.

Sitting in his old green Volvo Roman racked his brains, trying to think of the name of the company Jeff Ottway had worked for. It had been on the pocket of the overalls he was wearing when he died. 'Comtel', that was it—'Comtel'. Roman used his car phone to call the main switchboard at his radio station.

'Hello? Sharon? It's Mark Roman here. I'm in my car, can you look up a telephone number and street address for me, please. The name is Comtel. C-O-M-T-E-L. What's that? Hang on, let me just make a note of that. Thanks, Sharon, talk to you later.'

Roman then dialled the Comtel number and asked to speak to the personnel manager.

'Good afternoon. I'm sorry to disturb you. My name is Mark Roman . . . yes, that's right, from the radio. I'm making inquiries about a man named Jeff Ottway—I believe he worked for you, is that right? As an electrician? I see. I wanted to have a chat to someone who might have known him fairly well. What's that name again? Craig Connors? Jeff worked for him, did he? And would Mr Connors be available for a short chat if I called over now? Thank you, you've been most helpful.'

Roman hung up the phone, started the car, and headed in the direction of the Artarmon industrial area.

In Broughton Road, Artarmon, in between a printing company and a supplier of hydroponics equipment Roman found Comtel: their sign said

'Specialising in the Supply and Maintenance of High-voltage Generators.' A small notice indicated that the reception desk was on the first floor.

This time there was no gushing when Roman gave his name, but the receptionist kept looking at him until a short, bald-headed man in blue overalls appeared.

'Mr Roman, I'm Craig Connors.' They shook hands. 'Why don't we go back to my office to talk?'

Roman followed Connors through a swinging door, across a warehouse stacked high with large, wooden crates, past a work bench on which electrical equipment was being stripped down and repaired, to a small, glassed-in office at the back of the warehouse.

'Take a seat,' Connors said, waving his hand at the one spare seat in the room—a hard, upright, wooden chair. Connors himself sat behind a desk littered with papers.

'You wanted to know about Jeff Ottway?'

'That's right. I was the one who found his body on Tuesday morning. And, as a result, I seem to have become involved in finding out about Jeff, about what he was really like, and about what happened to him.'

'Have you spoken to his wife?'

'Yes. Caitlin is as puzzled by the last few days of Jeff's life as anybody else.'

'I see.'

'Well, he worked for you. Perhaps you saw a side of him Caitlin didn't. And if so, that would help.'

'I'm more than happy to help, if I can. What would you like to know?'

'To begin at the beginning: what exactly was Jeff's job here?'

'We sell emergency generators to . . . well, to anyone who might need an emergency generator. You know—hospitals, shopping malls, radio and television stations, police and fire stations. Those sorts of customers. And we provide a twenty-four hour maintenance and back-up service. Jeff was one of our maintenance electricians. As such he sometimes had to work shifts around the clock.'

'Like this week?'

'Exactly.'

'How long has he been with the firm?'

'At least ten years. A long time. Maybe twelve. Maybe it's even more than that. I'd have to look up his file to be certain.'

'Were you here when he came?'

'Sure. I hired him.'

'Do you remember where he had worked previously?'

'Some electrical installation company in . . . Rockdale, I think. Yeah, Rockdale.'

'And he came with references and so on?'

'Terrific references, as I recall.'

'So there was no sense of his leaving that company under a cloud?'

'My impression was—this is remembering back over twelve years, of course—was that they were sorry to lose him.'

'Why did he come then?'

'He wanted to live in this area. Or he had already bought a place in this area. Something like that it was.'

'And where else had he worked? Do you know?'

'That's easy—nowhere. That place in Rockdale

was his first employer. He did his apprenticeship there. Just there and here—the only two places he's ever worked.'

'And what can you tell me about him? Was he a good worker? Popular? How would you describe him?'

'Good at his job. But very quiet. And unambitious. He had brains. I tried to persuade him to do a university course part-time—electrical engineering. He wasn't interested.'

'He got on well with people here?'

'Very well. No problems.'

'What about his private life? Do you know anything about that?'

'He'd just got married when he first came here. But that broke up after a few years. And then a few years after that he married our receptionist.'

'That's Caitlin?'

'That's right.'

'He talked to me about having a heavy burden of guilt. Did he ever talk to you about that?'

'Never.'

'Any guesses as to what he felt so guilty about?'

'Nope. No idea.'

'Caitlin said he suffered badly from nightmares as well. Probably from the same source. And you have no idea what that could be?'

'None, I'm very much afraid. None at all. I'd help if I could, but . . .' He shrugged his shoulders.

'Thanks for your time, Mr Connors. You've helped to fill in the picture a little bit more.'

'Just so it helps to catch the bastard who killed Jeff, that's all.'

The longer that Roman pursued the puzzle of Jeff Ottway's murder, the more obsessed he was becoming with the nature of forgiveness, and the dangers of unforgiveness.

That night on the show the subject came up again.

'Phyllis from Bardwell Park is on the line. Evening, Phyllis.'

'Evening, Mark.'

'What did you want to talk about?'

'I wanted to take you back to a story you told on the show the other night.'

'Which story was this?'

'The one about a father and daughter. I think he was beaten up and she was raped by two men who broke into their house.'

'Yes, I remember.'

'And you said that both of them forgave their attackers, but then the father got upset when the men got a light sentence for the rape.'

'That's right. That's what happened.'

'Well, I've been thinking about it ever since you told the story. And I think that father's wrong.'

'In what way?'

'Well, it's a contradiction to say you forgive someone and then to want them to be punished. Surely that's not what real forgiveness means. I'm not saying he shouldn't campaign for a tougher sentence. It's just that it's not compatible with forgiving them at the same time.'

'Yes, I agree that it's a hard case. Since I told the story, I've remembered what Hugh Marsden said about it. That's my minister. He told the story last Sunday night. And he said the reason that it jars is that forgiveness means that the person who forgives carries the burden, the pain of forgiving.'

'Maybe that's what worries me about it.'

94

'Let me give you an example. If you owed me a hundred dollars and I said to you "I forgive the debt"—well, I couldn't then go and collect it, could I?'

'Of course not!'

'In that case forgiveness would cost me a hundred bucks. Forgiveness always costs something. And the person who pays the cost is the person who does the forgiving.'

'All of that makes sense to me, Mark,' said the caller. 'That's what I've always thought forgiveness means.'

'Exactly, Phyllis. So if you forgive someone for a hurt they've done you, that means you are bearing the burden of the hurt. Forgiving means pain-bearing, cost-bearing.'

'Which is why people find it so hard to forgive—they refuse to pay the price for someone else.'

'I guess so,' rumbled Roman. 'Let me tell a story that a mate of mine once told me. Is that okay?'

'Sure.'

'My mate John was driving to Melbourne. Around sunset he became tired and stopped in a tiny country town for a coffee—a "driver reviver" stop. As he got back into his car and pulled out from the gutter, a Range Rover with bull-bars came flying around the corner on the wrong side of the road, and smacked into John's car. John got out and looked at the damage—both headlights broken and the bumper pushed in. The Range Rover didn't have a scratch.

'John walked up to the driver of the four-wheel drive and said: "Alright, let's exchange details and give me the name of your insurance company— I'm in a hurry, I'm driving to Melbourne." A young

95

bloke got out of the Range Rover and said quietly, "I haven't got a licence. I'm only 15. This Range Rover belongs to a friend. I only drove it to impress a girl."

'So, John then had to decide what to do. He suggested to the kid that they both pop around to the police station. The kid pleaded with him not to. "Alright," said John, "I'll drive you to your place, we'll tell your father, and he can pay for the damage to my car." The kid, almost in tears, said that his father would beat the life out of him if he ever knew.

'The kid pleaded with John just to let him go, he had learned his lesson, and would never do anything as stupid as this again. What would you have done?'

'I don't know,' said Phyllis, 'that's a hard one.'

'Well,' said Roman, 'I'll tell you what John did—and to this day he doesn't know if it was the right thing to do. John let the kid go. He told him to drive the Range Rover straight back around the corner to his mate's place, and not to get behind the wheel again until he had a licence. John forgave him for his youthful stupidity.'

'I don't know that I would have been big enough to do that,' said the caller.

'Me neither!' Roman commented. 'Anyway, that wasn't the end of it. It couldn't be. There was still the damage to be paid for.'

'So what happened about that?'

'John paid for it himself. That's what forgiveness means. It means carrying the cost. It means paying the price. It means bearing the burden. That's what the one who does the forgiving does. You see,' added Roman, 'God can't simply forgive us—there

96

is still all the damage we have done to be paid for. That's why God sent Jesus to die on the cross—to pay for our damage, so that we could be forgiven.'

The next morning when Roman woke it was raining. He pulled back the curtains of his unit to see a grey washed world with thin streaks of rain trickling down the window, and fine, misty sheets of rain being swirled around by the wind off the harbour. Autumn had arrived with a vengeance.

Later, showered, shaved and dressed, Roman stood at the window sipping a hot cup of coffee and looking down at McDougall Street where people were struggling to control umbrellas as they hurried, heads down, against the rain. To be inside, and dry and warm, in such weather gave him an almost womb-like sense of comfort. He dragged himself away from the window reluctantly, in order to tackle a task he'd been putting off. He dialled the phone number Caitlin had given him for Jeff Ottway's parents.

'Hello?' a tremulous female voice answered.

'Mrs Ottway?'

'Speaking.'

'It's Mark Roman calling. Please accept my condolences on your loss. I got to know Jeff in the last few days of his life.'

There was a quiet sob on the end of the line.

'I would like to learn more about what Jeff was like. And I was wondering if I could call in and see you and your husband some time today?'

At this Beryl Ottway broke into uncontrolled sobbing. There was a series of clunks as the handset at the other end of the line was picked up by somebody else.

'Hello?' asked a gruff, male voice. 'Greg Ottway here. Who's calling please?'

'It's Mark Roman, Mr Ottway. I'm sorry if I upset your wife.'

'Not your fault, Mr Roman—Beryl's finding this very hard to cope with.'

'May I call in? To express my condolences, and have a chat, and so on?'

'Yes, of course. Any time. We're here all day.'

CHAPTER 7

Roman had to run to his car with his collar turned up, as fine, cold rain was still drizzling down. But by the time he hit General Holmes Drive not only had the rain stopped, most of the clouds had blown away.

He found himself driving on wet, shining roads under a blue, sunny sky. The sound of his tyres on the road changed as he drove through the tunnel under the airport runway, and then the whoosh returned as he emerged onto wet road at the other end. Driving towards Brighton-le-Sands, with Botany Bay on his left and a jumble of suburban houses on his right, made Roman remember his childhood. His parents had brought him here to swim when he was young. It was when he was in primary school, and his father was branch manager of a bank in Rockdale. In those days, Roman remembered, there were still trolley buses in Rockdale—double-decker green and yellow buses with rods running up to power lines over the road.

At Brighton he and his younger sister had swum in the sharkproof enclosure, played on the sand, and climbed on the old iron cannons that pointed out towards the bay.

Much was the same, but there was much that had changed as well, Roman noticed. An international hotel rose high above the Brighton-le-Sands shopping centre, and every second shop seemed to have become a seafood restaurant. As he continued south along The Grand Parade, Roman was aware of the number of blocks of units, many of them six to eight storeys high, that rose on his right-hand side.

He turned right into President Avenue, and then left into busy O'Connell Street. He passed older houses in dark, liver-coloured brick, interspersed with newer homes vaguely resembling Mediterranean villas, with balconies and columns, and some with small, white statues decorating the front lawn. O'Connell Street became Chuter Street, and Chuter Street became as wide as a boulevard—with a broad strip of grass and trees down the middle.

Slowing down to check the street names, he noticed how many of the houses had palm trees planted in their front gardens. Perhaps because they were so close to the sea, these suburbs on the shores of Botany Bay felt more like a part of the South Pacific than the rest of Sydney. Then Roman found the street he was looking for—Burlington.

It was a very mixed street. In amongst the large, modern bungalows in cream brick were older fibro houses. Many homes had double garages, and of those that didn't, most had power boats on trailers parked out front. Roman slowed down to read the numbers, and came to a halt in front a pale green painted fibro house. It looked immaculate—lawns manicured, gardens tidy, everything neat and in its place.

As he walked slowly to the front door, his heart felt as heavy as a lump of iron. This was not going to be easy. He wished that he had taken Jack Kingston's advice and not become involved.

He knocked. The sound seemed to echo inside. There was a long silence, then the sound of shuffling footsteps.

The door opened slowly to reveal a man in his late sixties, almost completely bald, with pale, blue eyes and a stunned, expressionless face.

'Ah, Mr Roman,' he said, before Roman could speak, 'it was good of you to come. I'm Greg Ottway.'

'Good morning,' replied Roman, lamely. 'Please accept my sympathies for the loss of your son.'

'Thank you,' said Ottway, and the two men shook hands.

Ottway ushered Roman into a narrow hallway wallpapered in muted pastel colours. Hanging on the wall was a circular mirror with a bevelled edge—of a style Roman had not seen since his childhood.

'This way,' said Ottway, leading Roman into a small lounge room, over-furnished with vinyl-covered sofa and chairs and what the department stores term an 'entertainment centre': a low bookshelf filled with TV, video, radio, CD player, and half a dozen books—mostly coffee table books dealing with the Second World War.

'Take a seat, Mr Roman . . .'

'Please call me Mark.'

'. . . Mark, then. I'll go and fetch Beryl—she'll want to meet you.'

Jeff Ottway's mother turned out to be a small woman, short and thin, her eyes red from tears, who seemed somehow shrunken by the blow that the death of her son had been. Roman shook her hand and repeated his condolences.

She kept a handkerchief crushed up in her left hand, and seemed reluctant to say much.

'How did you come to know our son, Mark?' asked Greg Ottway, once they were all seated.

'To begin with, he called my radio show.'

'He's quite a fan of yours,' said Ottway, and Roman noticed that he had spoken of Jeff in the present tense. 'When we got into debates he quite often quoted your opinions as being the final word on things. What did he ring about?'

'He said he was feeling guilty.'

'Guilty?' Ottway looked genuinely puzzled.

'Well, more than just feeling guilty. He said that he was carrying a heavy load of guilt. And he wanted to know how to deal with it.'

'No,' said Beryl Ottway quietly, 'not our Jeff. That can't be right.'

'Did he say what he was guilty of?' asked Greg.

'I'm afraid not,' admitted Roman. 'He was reluctant to talk about the details.'

'Did he ever say this to you?' asked Beryl, turning towards her husband.

'No, love. He never said anything like that to me. It seems so unlike Jeff.'

'He did talk about it as being a kind of secret. Something he had lived with for years, without telling anyone,' explained Roman.

'Could it have something to do with Lesley?' said Greg, turning to his wife.

Beryl Ottway said nothing, just shook her head in reply.

'We were unhappy when they broke up, Mark,' explained Greg. 'Jeff and Lesley almost grew up together. They went to the same schools—Ramsgate Primary and Rockdale High. They became boyfriend and girlfriend in their teens. We'd always assumed . . . well . . . no-one was surprised when they announced their engagement. And then, for a relationship like that to come to grief . . . well, it upset Beryl and me quite a lot, I can tell you.'

'We still see Lesley sometimes,' added Beryl. 'She pops in for a cup of tea when she's down this way visiting her mum. Even though she's re-married and got kiddies now.'

'That's why the marriage broke up, I reckon,' said Greg gruffly. 'They should have had kids.'

'When they were married five years and didn't, we thought they couldn't,' Beryl said, still talking very quietly, a puzzled expression on her face. 'But now Lesley has kiddies of her own, and Jeff has dear little Eleanor. So they could have.'

'It would have saved their marriage,' added Greg.

'Well,' rumbled Roman slowly, 'it might have been something to do with Lesley. The guilt, I mean. I should talk to her. Can you give me an address or phone number?'

'I can give you both,' said Greg, standing up and walking briskly out of the room, apparently pleased to have something to do.

In his absence Roman and Beryl Ottway looked at each other for a moment. She had a wary, guarded look in her eyes.

'Jeff had nothing to be guilty about!' she said, to break the silence.

'Quite possibly—but he *felt* he had. And that's what was troubling him.'

'He was a good boy,' she added firmly.

Just then her husband returned carrying a plastic teledex, a small notebook, and a stub of pencil. He sat down, clicked open the teledex, and copied an address and phone number onto a page of the notebook.

'While you're going,' Roman said, 'could you add the name of Jeff's first employer, please?'

'Sure.'

When he had finished scribbling his note, Greg Ottway tore it out and passed it over to Roman.

'Thank you. And you're quite sure Jeff never said anything to either of you about a sense of guilt?'

Greg and Beryl looked at each other, then looked back towards Roman and both slowly shook their heads.

'What about when he was young? Some kids get up to pretty wild things when they're teenagers . . .'

'Not Jeff!' interrupted Beryl.

'He was always such a good, solid, reliable kid, Mark. He left high school and went straight into an apprenticeship with a local firm of electrical fitters. They were very sorry to lose him when he left.'

'Yes, tell me about that. Why did he leave?'

'We don't know,' said Greg, shaking his head. 'We could never quite understand that, could we, love?' he added, turning to Beryl.

'He just wanted to better himself,' suggested Beryl in a quiet voice.

'But he was doing so well here,' her husband insisted. 'It almost seemed like a whim. Unless it had something to do with the accident? Remember, love? We wondered about that at the time.'

'What accident?' asked Roman.

'His best mate was in a hit-and-run accident. Was in hospital for months afterwards.'

'Jeff was very shaken by that,' Beryl added, with a nod of her head.

'He'd always been a happy-go-lucky sort of bloke before David's accident,' Greg explained. 'I think it pulled him up with a shock. Made him realise that life is . . . well, not safe. If you know what I mean.'

'It reminded him of his own mortality,' rumbled Roman.

'Something like that. After all, David nearly died, didn't he, love?'

'Almost died,' echoed his wife 'Jeff found it impossible to visit David when he was in hospital. Jeff can't cope with death, and injury, and hospitals—says he can't stand the smell of them.'

'When David came out of hospital they had a bit of a blue about that,' Greg said, 'about Jeff not visiting. But they made it up again. They must have, because David came to Jeff's wedding.'

'So this accident upset Jeff. Can you think of anything else?'

'Anything else? Well, he was upset about Peter's death, wasn't he, love?'

Beryl nodded her head.

'Tell me,' Roman said.

'This was a bloke from Jeff's work, a good friend of Jeff's. Got swept off rocks when he was fishing. They didn't find his body for three days.'

'And when did Jeff leave and move over to Chatswood?'

'Artarmon,' corrected Beryl. 'That's where he and Lesley went to live just after the wedding. Jeff moved to Chatswood when his marriage broke up.'

'Did he ever mention nightmares to you? Persistent nightmares?'

'No . . .' Greg answered, shaking his head slowly as he spoke.

'Lesley told me about them,' interrupted Beryl.

'What did she say?' Roman enquired.

'Only that he had bad nightmares occasionally. Woke up in a sweat and couldn't get back to sleep for hours. She said that once he woke up screaming.'

'What were the nightmares about?'

'Jeff wouldn't tell her.'

'I'd better ask her about that,' mumbled Roman, more to himself than the Ottways.

'But here we are talking away, and being very inhospitable,' said Greg. 'Would you like a cup of tea or coffee?'

'I don't want to put you to any trouble.'

'No trouble.'

'Well, only if you're having a cup.'

'It's about time I had a cup of coffee,' Greg said, nodding his head as if to emphasise the words. 'What do you say, love?' he added, turning to his wife, 'three cups of coffee, eh?'

Without a word Beryl rose to her feet and left the room.

'Sad business,' Greg said gruffly, looking down at his slippered feet and shaking his head. 'It really pulls a bloke up when his son . . . thirty years younger . . . goes before he does.'

For several moments there was a heavy silence in the room, and then Greg spoke again. 'This business he rang you about, Mark—do you think it could have anything to do with Jeff being killed?'

106

'It's certainly possible. To tell the truth—it looks more than likely to me. The police don't agree with me. They think it was a burglary gone wrong.'

'Burglary! What's Jeff got that's worth stealing? He doesn't own a lot. Never been paid much. And it's expensive to raise a young kiddie these days.'

'I take it Caitlin doesn't work?'

'No. And quite right too. While Ellie is so little.'

'So if it wasn't a burglary,' Roman prompted, 'it could have something to do with this matter he rang me about.'

'That's what I'm thinking,' Greg agreed, dropping his voice, 'and there was something, Mark. I just didn't want to say it in front of Jeff's mum.'

Roman looked expectantly, and, after a pause, Greg continued.

'It was about the time Jeff re-married. He was feeling pretty pleased with himself at the time. I was out in the garage making a coffee table for Jeff and Caitlin's new home unit. I do a bit of wood turning, you see. Anyway, Jeff was there, and the conversation got a bit serious—talking about the meaning of life, all that stuff. You know what I mean.'

'Yes, I do.'

'Well, Jeff sort of stopped in the middle of this chat and said he had something important to say. Something he'd never told anyone. He was sort of coughing and spluttering, finding it hard to get started, when Beryl called us inside for afternoon tea. The moment passed. He never mentioned it again, and neither did I. So there was something, Mark—something he never told me or his mother about.'

'I see.'

Beryl returned just then with three cups of coffee and a small plate of biscuits on a tray. As she handed out the cups Roman noticed that the tray was decorated with a reproduction of an Albert Namatjira painting. He suddenly had a feeling that Beryl and Greg probably had a collection of decorative teaspoons, and tea towels printed with 'Greetings from Broken Hill.'

The biscuits were Iced Vo-Vos, which Roman hadn't eaten since his school days. Somehow the drive to Ramsgate was turning into a journey back in time—back to school uniforms, simple pleasures, and unbounded hope.

'How did Jeff and Caitlin get on? Was he happy?' Roman asked.

'Yes . . . yes, as far as I know,' replied Greg carefully. 'We never saw any signs of trouble, did we, love?' he added, checking with his wife.

Greg nodded thoughtfully to himself for a moment, and then continued, 'especially since Ellie was born. Jeff was real pleased to be a dad. And Ellie's such a good little kiddie. I think Jeff was happy in his marriage. As much as anyone is ever happy in this world. Not like with Lesley. Towards the end, just before the break-up, it was quite embarrassing when they came to visit. Wasn't it, love?'

Beryl nodded and sipped her tea.

'They'd taken to having their arguments in front of other people,' Greg said, squirming uncomfortably in his seat at the memory. 'I mean to say, that's not right, is it? I mean, we just never knew which way to look. In that sense when they

108

separated it was a bit of relief. It's just a pity it ever came to that.'

Roman finished his coffee and stood up to leave.

'Thank you for making me so welcome,' he said, 'and again—I'm so sorry about your loss.'

They both escorted him to the front door.

'Find out what you can, Mark,' said Greg earnestly as he opened the door. 'We've got to know. If the police just say it was an unknown burglar and forget about it, it'll never be finished, never be over for us. If you know what I mean.'

Roman said he did and shook hands with both of them, then walked briskly to his car, looking back as he was unlocking the driver's door to wave goodbye. They were still standing in the doorway, but they weren't looking at him. Greg had turned his back on the street, his head was lowered and his shoulders were heaving spasmodically. He was crying. Tiny Beryl had her arms around him and was comforting him, as if he were an over-grown child.

Roman started the engine and drove out of Burlington Street in a daze. By the time he came to his senses, he was driving south down Chuter Street again—going in the wrong direction. He came to a sudden decision not to head straight back to the city but to stop and eat some lunch while watching the waters of Botany Bay.

It all came flooding back to him.

Ramsgate swimming pool, when Roman was young, was quite unlike tiled, modern swimming pools. It was more like a fun fair. For a start, there was nothing remotely resembling an Olympic-sized pool. Instead, there was an odd mixture of concrete pools of assorted sizes. And around these pools there were distorting mirrors, and slippery dips into the water. And the water itself was real sea water (presumably pumped each day from Botany Bay), not the chlorinated stuff that kids swim in today.

And then Roman remembered the food. It was the only place that he knew of, when he was child, where he could get pineapple fritters and banana fritters—dripping with cholesterol and absolutely delicious.

He parked the old green Volvo in Ramsgate Road and walked across the street to the small shopping centre. He bought a copy of the *Daily Telegraph-Mirror* at the newsagents, and browsed around the snack bars looking for lunch. Then he saw them, at a hot food bar: pineapple fritters. Suddenly he felt like an eight year old again. He bought two of the greasy fritters, and skipped across The Grand Parade, in between the traffic, to the park that bordered the bay.

Roman walked to the sea wall, and found that it was high tide. There was no sand visible, and the small waves of the bay were lapping with a delicious musical sound against the wall.

He opened up the paper bag and bit into one of the pineapple fritters. Almost instantly he regretted it. What had changed over the intervening years? The pineapple fritters? Or himself? He put the remains of his 'lunch' back into the paper bag, and threw it into a nearby garbage bin. Then he wiped the grease off his fingers with his handkerchief, and began to stroll, at a leisurely pace, along the top of the sea wall, above the gently lapping waves.

He came to the place that had once been the

Ramsgate Baths. The old swimming pool had only been a block or so from the bay, and in addition there was this swimming area—a shark-proof enclosure in the bay itself. The framework was a timber semi-circle, like a post-and-rail fence, and between the posts were rusted iron bars to keep the sharks out while letting the water surge freely back and forth.

It was falling down now, and permanent cyclone fencing prevented public access to the concrete steps into the old bathing area. Roman was sorry he had come. He wanted to remember it as it was, not in its present dilapidated condition. He turned his back on the water, and marched briskly back to his car.

Before he started the engine, he pulled the scrap of notepaper out of his pocket that Greg had given him. Lesley's married (or re-married) name was Gray. He dialled the number. It was answered almost at once.

'Hello?'

'Mrs Gray?'

'Speaking. Who's that, please?'

'My name is Mark Roman.'

'From the radio?'

'That's right.'

'Have I won a prize, or something?'

'I'm afraid not. I'm calling about your first husband—Jeff Ottway.'

'Oh, yes. How stupid of me. I read about it in the paper. You found his body, didn't you?'

'That's right.'

'Well, what can I do for you?'

'May I call in and have a chat to you about Jeff?'

111

'I've had no contact with him for seven years now. You do realise that?'

'Still, I'd like to talk with you about Jeff if I may?'

'Why? If you don't mind me being direct.'

'No, I don't mind. It's just that I would—we would—like to understand why Jeff died.'

'Who's "we"?'

'I've just come from Jeff's parents.'

'You've seen Beryl and Greg?'

'That's right.'

'And they're happy for you to go around asking questions?'

'More than that—Greg encouraged me.'

'Well, in that case . . . come over if you want. But I doubt that I can tell you anything useful.'

'Thank you. I'll come over now, if I may.'

'Certainly. Do you have the address?'

Roman assured her that he had, and, after doing some calculations in his head, told her when to expect him.

Lesley Gray lived in Five Dock, in Preston Avenue, only a short block from Hen and Chicken Bay. During the drive across Pyrmont Bridge Roman checked in with his radio station.

'Sharon love,' said Roman to the main switchboard operator, 'any messages for me?'

'Allan in sales said to tell you that Robinson's Tyre Service have renewed their contract, and he wants to talk to you about recording some new ads.'

'Okay. Anything else?'

'A listener rang with a message. He was most particular that I get it down word for word.'

'What's the message?'

'It says: "Find out why Craig Connors hated Jeff Ottway." That's all. Does it make any sense to you?'

'It makes sense alright. Did the caller leave a name?'

'No. It was good old anonymous again.'

'A man or a woman?'

'A man.'

'Young? Old?'

'I dunno. Middle-aged, I guess.'

'Thanks, Sharon love. I'll follow it up.'

By the time he'd hung up he was driving down Lyons Road, passing a small community radio station on his right, followed by a bowling green and clubhouse. Then he crossed over the Great North Road intersection and turned right into Preston Road. He followed the road as it curved around, until he came to the number he was looking for.

Lesley Gray lived in a two-storey, house that looked across playing fields onto the waves of the bay. Lesley had done better than her electrician ex-husband.

Roman rang the door bell and heard a musical chime echo deep within the house. A minute later the door was opened by a tall, slim brown-haired young woman, nursing a baby on one hip.

'So,' she said, 'it really is Mark Roman. Ever since the phone call I've been wondering if it was someone who could impersonate your voice just pulling my leg.'

'It really is me, I'm afraid,' Roman said. 'Besides which—no-one can do my voice.'

Lesley Gray stepped back and invited Roman inside.

113

'Tea? Coffee?' she said.

'No thanks. If I drink any more coffee I'll squelch when I walk.'

She led the way into a large, L-shaped lounge room with floor-to-ceiling glass looking out over the park and the water.

'Nice place you have here,' Roman remarked.

'We like it,' said Lesley, as she put the baby down on the thick pile carpet, and gave it a squeaky toy to play with.

'Materially, you've done better than Jeff.'

'Malcolm—my husband—is a real estate agent. He's very good at his job. We've done well.'

'As I told you on the phone, I'm trying to, well, understand Jeff—and understand why he was killed.'

'And, as I told you, we've had no contact for such a long time that I'm sure I can't help.'

'What about his character? Surely you can help me with that? What was Jeff like?'

'For most of the time I knew him he was a quiet, serious boy. That's what attracted me to him way back in high school,' said Lesley, her eyes becoming misty as the memories took over. 'He was so much more . . . I don't know, grown-up maybe, than all the other boys. He seemed very mature to me then. Sensible. Not a yahoo. If you know what I mean?'

'I think I do. You said: "For most of the time" that you knew him—does that mean he changed?'

'That's what went wrong. Greg and Beryl were upset when we divorced. But they hadn't seen the change in Jeff. I had. I lived with him.'

'What change?'

'He'd always been the quiet type, but after he

114

changed it was more than that. He became sullen, almost sulky. Some days it was hard to get a word out of him. He'd eat his dinner in silence, then he'd watch TV in silence. You can't have a relationship with someone who won't talk to you.'

'What lay behind his silence?'

'I thought it was me.'

'You? Why?'

'Because it started when we got married. The honeymoon was fun. But when he went back to work and we settled into a routine he just slowly sank into this awful silence. When he wanted to leave our little flat in Ramsgate and move over to the other side of the harbour I agreed. I thought a move might snap him out of it. We changed our home. Jeff changed his job. But it didn't cure him. If anything the silences got worse.'

'Did you talk to him about it?'

'Endlessly. But he wouldn't talk to me. I tried to jolly him out of it. I tried to be sympathetic. Nothing worked. In the end I found myself nagging him about it, and that's when the marriage fell apart.'

'Did Jeff ever hurt you? Emotionally? Or physically?'

'Hurt me! That's ridiculous! He was as gentle as a lamb—and about as boring! Living with Jeff was as dangerous as living with a statue. After the divorce, that's what attracted me to Malcolm. Malcolm never stops talking—and it's wonderful. He's company for me, and poor old Jeff never was.'

'You said you blamed yourself for his sullenness: do you still think it was your fault?'

'To be absolutely honest, Mr Roman, I haven't

a clue. I never understood then, and I still don't understand now.'

'Could there have been any connection between his silences and his nightmares?'

'Who told you about Jeff's nightmares?' snapped Lesley.

'Caitlin, and Beryl Ottway,' Roman explained.

'Oh. I see. Well, I guess there might have been a connection. But if so, I never found out what it was.'

'Tell me about the nightmares. What were they like?'

'Just nightmares, I guess. Like any other nightmares. He used to toss and turn and mumble to himself, and then wake up dripping with sweat and badly shaken.'

'What did he mumble about?'

'I tried very hard to understand, Mr Roman, believe me I did. To help Jeff I tried to play at being Sherlock Holmes, but I could never make out a word. It was like listening to a drunken man slurring and mumbling. None of the words were ever clear enough to understand.'

'Did you ask Jeff what the nightmares were about?'

'Of course. And of course it did me no good. He just retreated into his sullen silence again. After a bad run with the nightmares he was always especially distant and withdrawn.'

'When Jeff called me he talked about carrying a burden of guilt. He said he'd been carrying it for years. It probably goes back to the time when you knew him. Do you know what he had to be guilty about?'

'Jeff? Guilty? He was harmless. Silent, sullen,

withdrawn—but quite harmless. Jeff had nothing to be guilty about, of that I'm certain. It was a figment of his imagination. It must have been. He hadn't got into trouble in high school. Or when he was an apprentice. He was the sort of kid every mum wants. Maybe that was the trouble. If he'd been a bit more lively and outgoing our marriage would have survived. Perhaps being such a self-absorbed, introspective sort of bloke he blew something up in his imagination—some small thing.'

'Perhaps,' said Roman doubtfully, recalling the confrontation, the 'vicious' confrontation, Jeff had reported to him.

'I really don't think I can tell you anything else,' Lesley said, rising to her feet.

'You've been a help,' Roman said, as he followed her to the front door. 'Thank you for your time.'

'By the way,' remarked Lesley, as she held the door open, 'what's Caitlin like?'

'You never met her?'

'Never even seen her. What's she like?'

'Quite pretty. Short black hair. Lavender blue eyes. I've only met her once myself. She seemed very nice. They have a little daughter, you know.'

'Yes, I know. Beryl told me.'

As the door closed behind him Roman looked at his watch. Almost four o'clock. If he hurried he could be outside Comtel when it closed for the day. And he wanted to be there to catch Craig Connors as he left work. If the anonymous phone tip was correct, Connors had lied to him. And that lie, thought Roman, might be the key to unlock the whole mystery.

CHAPTER 8

Roman parked the old green Volvo in a loading zone on the opposite side of the street to the Comtel building. He hadn't been there long when a trickle of workers began to emerge as the warehouse closed down for the day.

Craig Connors was among the last to leave. As soon as he saw Connors emerge from the main door, Roman leapt out of his car and walked across the street on an interception course.

'Craig!' called out Roman.

Connors looked around, startled. When he saw who was calling him he beamed.

'Mark,' he said, 'nice to see you again.'

Then he turned to the two men who had walked out of the building with him and said, 'Brian, Mike, this is my mate, Mark Roman.'

Roman shook hands all around. He was used to being treated as 'my friend the radio star' and was quite prepared to let Connors show off for a while, if that would help to get some answers later.

'What can I do for you, Mark?' asked Connors.

'I want another chat about Jeff Ottway.'

'Sure. Sure. I was just going to my regular watering hole for a drink. Why don't you join me?'

'Okay. Where do you drink?'

'The Great Northern. My car's just around the

corner. What about I meet you there in . . . say, five minutes?'

'Five minutes. Alright,' agreed Roman.

'I'll see you blokes tomorrow,' Connors added, turning back towards his work mates. They both looked put out—as if they had been expecting an invitation to join Craig and Roman at the pub.

'Oh, sure, okay. See ya tomorrow,' one of them murmured.

Roman and Connors split up and each drove in his own car to the Great Northern Hotel. By the time Roman had found a parking spot in Mowbray Road and walked back to the pub, Connors was already waiting for him in the public bar.

Connors ordered a beer and Roman a Claytons and soda, then they took their drinks to a relatively quiet corner.

'Cheers,' grinned Connors, as he took a drink and licked his lips, and then said, 'now, what can I do for you?'

'Tell me more about Jeff Ottway. And about his friends—and enemies,' rumbled Roman.

'I've already told you everything I know,' complained Connors.

'Everything?'

'Everything!'

'Tell me who at Comtel didn't get on with Jeff.'

'No-one. I told you before. Jeff was a quiet bloke who got on well with everyone.'

'Who hated him, then?'

'Hated him? No-one.'

'Except you. Right?'

'What do you mean—"except me"? Who's been telling stories?'

119

'It doesn't matter who's been telling them. What I want to know is the truth behind them.'

'There isn't any. Someone's been telling you a pack of lies.'

'"Find out why Craig Connors hated Jeff Ottway." Why would someone say that me if it wasn't true?'

'Who said it?'

'Doesn't matter. Is it true? *That* matters!'

'Well, it isn't true. End of discussion.'

Roman took a quiet sip on his drink, and then asked, 'Why didn't you invite your mates to join us for a drink?'

'Why should I?'

'I think they expected you to.'

'Well, tough luck for them!' Connors snapped.

'Don't get edgy.'

'I'm not getting edgy.'

'Well, what is it then? Guilt?'

'What have I got to be guilty about?'

'Perhaps your hatred for Jeff Ottway. Perhaps lying to me.'

'Garbage! You're not the police. I don't have to answer any questions if I don't want to.'

'Of course you don't. But I thought you wanted to help find Jeff's killer.'

'That's not your job. The cops'll do that. Leave it to the wallopers.'

'And will you be more honest with them than you've been with me?'

'Who says I've been dishonest?' Connors' voice was getting louder with each exchange. People nearby were starting to look at him.

'Why didn't you invite your mates for a drink?

120

Were you afraid they'd say something about your relationship with Jeff?'

'Just shove off! Shove off! You've got no right to ask me any questions. And I don't want to talk to you anymore!'

With that Connors pushed back his chair and stood up. He elbowed his way through the crowd around the bar and without a backward glance disappeared through the pub door. Roman finished his drink in thoughtful silence, and then followed him.

In a long and busy day, Roman realised, he had given no thought to doing prep for that night's show. He drove back home, microwaved a shepherd's pie, and hurriedly scanned the newspapers while he ate, looking for topics to talk about. Half an hour later, with a bunch of newspaper clippings stuffed into his pocket, he drove to the radio station.

'Where have you been?' asked Andrew Gardner as Roman stepped out of the lift.

'I've been busy all day. Why do you ask?'

'The rozzers have been around the place looking for you.'

'The police? Did they say what they wanted?'

'They said they'd been to your apartment, but you weren't there, so they came here.'

'Did this policeman give his name?' Roman asked.

'McDermott,' replied Andrew.

'That stands to reason. He's about as subtle as a car crash.'

At that moment the program director, Tom Mutch, appeared in the corridor.

'Mark,' he called, 'can I see you in my office for a moment?'

'Sure.'

As Roman stepped into the PD's office Mutch said, 'Close the door behind you, Mark.'

This was such an unusual request that Roman raised his eyebrows in astonishment.

'Just close it!' snapped Mutch. 'And take a seat.'

'What's this all about, Tom?' asked Roman as he pulled up a chair.

'I've had a very rude, very irritating policeman hanging around this radio station for much of the afternoon, and I want to know what's going on.'

'Detective McDermott's been here. Andrew told me.'

'But why, Mark? Why is he so interested in you? He gives the impression that he's investigating *you*! This didn't happen last time . . .'

'In the Escobar murder case? No, it didn't. But then, McDermott wasn't on that case.'

'What's this McDermott got on you, Mark? What's going on? Are you more involved in this than it seems?'

'It's not a matter of what McDermott has on me,' Roman explained slowly and patiently, 'but rather what he has against me.'

'Whadda ya mean?'

'McDermott took a dead set against me from the moment he laid eyes on me. I didn't provoke it, Tom, I swear I didn't. I don't know what it's all about. My best guess is that McDermott has got a hang-up about bringing celebrities down a peg or two.'

'And that's all it is?'

'That's all it is.'

122

'You're sure? Sure there's no scandal about to break over this radio station?' queried Mutch, his brow furrowed in anxiety.

'No, Tom—you can relax,' said Roman soothingly.

'Alright then. If you say so. But I'll tell you one thing for free—*you* can't afford to relax!'

'Why so?'

'This McDermott character is on your case good and proper—so you can expect an unpleasant time over the next day or two.'

'Thanks for the warning, Tom. I'm a big bloke; I can roll with the punches. When McDermott doesn't get anywhere he'll give up and go and bother someone else.'

'I hope you're right—for your sake.'

For the next two hours Roman sat in his tiny office, banging out editorials on his computer terminal, and sorting out the bundle of paper in his studio folder. Then, as nine o'clock approached he made a cup of strong coffee and wandered into the studio.

He had decided that for the time being he, and probably the listeners as well, had had enough of heavy topics, and so, inspired by his morning visit to Ramsgate, Roman had decided to do a 'nostalgia' program.

He kicked off the show with a ramble through the boyhood memories Ramsgate had awoken for him, and then invited the listeners to call with memories of their own childhoods. It was a topic that always worked well, and for that reason Roman didn't like to do it too often. But tonight seemed like the right night. The switchboard lit up

123

like a demented Christmas tree, and the show was jammed with calls from beginning to end.

Less than an hour into the show, shortly before the ten o'clock news, the computer showed 'Dylan of Chatswood' as the next caller.

'Evening, Dylan,' Roman said, as he took the line.

'It's me,' came an excited voice down the phone line. 'You said I could call.'

'I did indeed, Dylan,' rumbled Roman. 'What did you want to talk about?'

'About what you were saying at the start of the show. You know, about the old Ramsgate swimming pool?'

'Right.'

'You forgot to mention the monkeys. Beside one of the pools there was a wire cage—a big cage—that had a colony of small monkeys in it.'

'You're quite right!' said Roman with delight. 'Until this moment I'd forgotten the monkeys. But yes, I remember now. We used to poke chips and scraps of food through the wire to feed them.'

This call provoked another, just after the ten o'clock bulletin.

'You and Dylan remembered the monkeys,' said 'Ruth of Rockdale' in a quavering, elderly voice, 'but you both forgot the birds. There were two cages—the size of walk-in aviaries—side by side. One of them contained the monkeys and the other was full of tropical birds.'

'Can you remember what sort of birds?' Roman asked.

'No, I'm afraid I can't, Mark. Perhaps one of the other listeners can.'

That provoked a further flood of memories and

124

calls. By midnight, when the show ended, Mark was pleased. It had been three hours of very entertaining radio, and, for him, a break from heavy subjects and heavy arguments.

The next morning Roman was woken by a ringing telephone. He glanced at his bedside clock: eight a.m. For someone who didn't fall asleep until two a.m. that was too early. He tried to bury his head under the pillow, but he could still hear it, and it wouldn't stop ringing.

Finally he forced himself to get out of bed and stagger to the phone.

'Hello?'

'Good morning, Mr Roman, it's Detective McDermott here. We need to talk to you at Chatswood Police Station today. Could you be here in, say, half an hour.'

'No, I couldn't,' Roman growled, feeling a flash of irritation, and doing his best to control it. 'You know I work a late night shift, and you have deliberately rung early to wake me. I'm sorry, but I won't be at Chatswood Police Station in half an hour.'

There was a long silence at the other end of the phone line.

'Very well, Mr Roman,' McDermott said at last, 'if that's how you want to play it—I'll just have to come and get you.'

'And what if I go back to sleep? What will you do then—smash down the door?'

'If you really want to prevent the police from executing their duty, then that's a decision for you to make, Mr Roman,' threatened McDermott.

'I will do everything I can to get some more sleep,' Roman said quickly, 'including calling friends in the radio station newsroom and on the newspapers to give them a story about police harassment.'

'There's no point in being stupid about this, Roman.'

'I think you're the one who's being foolish, Mr McDermott. If it amuses you to make life difficult for me, go ahead—I can't stop you. All I can promise is that it won't remain a secret. And in the end you might only succeed in making life difficult for yourself.'

'Get some clothes on, Roman!' McDermott snarled, 'I'm on my way with two uniformed officers and I intend bringing you back to the station for questioning right now!

There was a loud clunk as McDermott slammed the phone down.

For about a minute Roman stood in his pyjamas in the middle of his tiny living room, trying to decide what to do. It was obvious that he wasn't going to get any more sleep, so he showered and shaved and dressed.

When he had done this he looked out the front window of his apartment. Ten minutes had passed since the phone call, and there was still no sign of a police car.

'Well,' he murmured to himself, 'I'll stick to my morning routine—until something else happens.'

He pulled on a jacket, since the wind whistling in off the harbour was bound to be quite cool, locked up the apartment, and set out on his usual morning walk to the Milsons Point shops.

'You're early this morning,' said the newsagent, as Roman bought his copy of the *Daily Telegraph-Mirror*.

'Couldn't sleep,' said Roman, without explaining why he couldn't sleep. And then, feeling in no hurry to return to his apartment, he settled down in a coffee shop, ordered a cappuccino and a hot breakfast, and started to read the paper.

It was an hour later that he left the coffee shop to walk slowly back to his apartment. At the point where Winslow Street joins McDougall Street he stopped, and cautiously looked around the corner. No police car. With his paper tucked underneath his arm, he walked briskly back to his apartment.

But when he unlocked the front door, he discovered a sheet of notepaper on the floor—clearly it had been pushed underneath the door while he was out.

'Call Chatswood Police Station immediately you return,' the note read; and it was signed, 'D.C. McDermott.' The word 'immediately' was underlined.

Roman, however, decided to interpret 'immediately' in his own terms. He suspected that he might be tied up for a long time once he fell into McDermott's hands. With that thought in mind, he decided to do his prep for that night's show before he did anything else.

An hour later he had a folder full of press clippings, and some scribbled notes for editorials. With those preparations he could do the show even if he arrived at the studio just five minutes before air time. Roman decided he could legitimately delay the inevitable no longer, and dialled the number of the Police Station.

'Chatswood Police.'

'Detective McDermott, please.'

'Hold the line please, sir.'

Pause. Click.

'McDermott speaking.'

'Good morning, Mr McDermott, it's Mark Ro . . .'

'I know who it is! If you know what's good for you, you'll get yourself into this station within fifteen minutes.'

'Otherwise . . . ?'

'Otherwise I'm issuing a press release saying that you are wanted to assist police with their inquiries. We can both play the media game, Mr Smart Aleck Roman!'

Clunk. The phone had been slammed down at the other end.

Before leaving, Roman called his radio station and asked for the newsroom.

'News.'

'Is Brian Farrell there, please?'

'He's right beside me, Mark. Hang on, I'll pass over the phone.'

Mark waited a few seconds.

'G'day, Mark, it's Brian. What can I do for you?'

'Let me tell you a story, Brian,' said Roman, and he narrated, in detail, the morning's events.

'Do you want me to do anything about it?' asked Farrell. 'I could run the story, or I could talk to one of my mates at Police Headquarters.'

'No, don't do anything right at the moment. I just wanted you to know, so that if McDermott carries out his threat of a media release, you can put it into context.'

'Understood. Oh, and by the way, you shouldn't worry about this. McDermott's just playing the bully for his own amusement. I'd say he's one of the old-school cops, and there are not many of them left. He won't get much support if this goes wobbly on him.'

'That's good to know,' murmured Roman. 'Oh, and one other thing—don't tell Tom Mutch any of this. He'll have kittens and start screaming at people. There's no need to worry him unnecessarily.'

'Understood. I'll just keep a watching brief. And you look after yourself.'

Ten minutes later Roman parked his car in the Grace Brothers car park, and walked down to the Chatswood Police Station in Archer Street.

'Would you tell Detective Constable McDermott that Mark Roman is here to see him, please?' he announced at the front desk.

The young uniformed constable looked at him twice, as if to make sure that he was indeed *the* Mark Roman, and then disappeared through a doorway.

A moment later he returned.

'If you'd just step this way, please, Mr Roman,' he said, holding a door open, 'Detective McDermott is expecting you.'

'I'm sure he is!' Roman muttered to himself under his breath.

The door opened into a corridor, at the end of which McDermott stood waiting, arms folded, legs apart.

'Very good of you to spare us a little of your valuable time,' sneered the detective, adding as an aside, 'That's all, constable. I'll take over now.'

McDermott waited until the uniformed man had disappeared, then he opened a door labelled 'Interview Room'.

'In here, Roman,' he snapped.

Inside was a plain wooden table, and four hard, stiff-backed chairs.

'Take a seat, Roman—I'll be back in a moment.'

McDermott closed the door behind him as he left. As an experiment Roman tried the door knob. As he expected, it was locked. He took a seat in one of the uncomfortable chairs, leaned back, closed his eyes, and tried to relax. It was obvious that McDermott intended to keep him waiting as long as possible.

The minutes crawled by, until Roman's wrist-watch showed that they added up to an hour. Then an hour and a half.

Eventually, the lock clicked, and the door re-opened.

'Sorry to keep you waiting so long, Roman,' said McDermott, with mock courtesy, 'I'm sure that big stars like you are not used to being kept waiting. That's true, isn't it?'

'How can I help you with your inquiries, Mr McDermott?' asked Roman gently.

'It's true, isn't it?' McDermott snapped. 'You expect to be fawned over all the time, don't you Roman?'

It was not a question that needed an answer, so Roman didn't supply one.

'Don't you?' McDermott half-bellowed.

'How can I help with your investigation, Mr McDermott?' said Roman, with great self-control. 'I'm here to help in any way I can.'

'You bet you are!' snarled the detective.

A long hostile silence followed, broken at last by the policeman.

'Firstly, I want you to explain why you've been interviewing all the witnesses in this case.'

'All the . . . ?'

'The witnesses! You know who I mean—Ottway's wife, and neighbours, and work mates, and parents. Why are you sticking your nose into police business?'

Roman thought carefully about his reply. This Neanderthal would not comprehend his need to *understand* the springs of violence that take a human life. So he fell back on the old media excuse.

'I'm a radio man, Mr McDermott. This is not only a murder case, it's also a story. I'm doing the work of an investigative *reporter*—not an investigative *detective*. Okay?'

'No, not okay!'

'Well, I'm sorry about that. But in our democratic society, it is allowed. And so I'm doing it. And that's all there is to it.'

'No, that isn't all—not by a long chalk it isn't!'

'What do you mean?'

'I mean that you are using your media work as a cover. What you're really doing is muddying the waters.'

'Muddying the waters?'

'Don't repeat what I say!'

'But I don't understand . . .'

'Oh, you understand alright. Don't play the dummy with me. The only question is: why? Why would a big radio star like you want to muddy the waters in a small-time murder like this? There's only one answer, isn't there?'

'You'd better tell me, because I'll never guess,' rumbled Roman, momentarily allowing his temper to make him sarcastic.

'You've got something to hide, haven't you,

Roman? That's what it's all about, isn't it? I don't know what it is you're covering up, but I intend to find out.'

'Is that it, then? Is that what you wanted to tell me? Because if it is, I'll toddle off now.'

'No! That's not all! And you're not going anywhere!'

'In that case, I'd like to talk to Detective Marsh, please?'

'It's the DS's day off today. Sorry about that. No fan club here for you today, Roman. Just me.'

There was a long, hostile silence, while McDermott paced back and forth in the small room.

'Let's go back to the beginning, Roman,' he said, at last.

'What beginning?'

'Your relationship to the deceased.'

'What about it?'

'Tell me all about it.'

'I already have. He was a listener, and a caller, to my show. He asked me for some advice. I tried to help. End of relationship. '

'You're lying!'

'I'm not. What I've just told you is the simple truth.'

'Convince me!'

'How? I don't think you want to be convinced. Or to listen. What can I say that will convince you that I am telling the truth?'

McDermott ignored this question, and took off on another tack.

'Why are you really digging into this case, Roman? Why are you upsetting all these people? Why are you asking so many questions? What do you hope to achieve?'

'What do *you* hope to achieve with your investigation, Mr McDermott?'

'A conviction!' shot back the detective, 'Which is more than you will ever achieve with this amateurish meddling in our inquiries!'

'Is that what's really bothering you? The fact that I won't accept the "burglar theory" that you and Marsh are so fond of? Is that what bothers you? Is it that I keep insisting there is more to this case than you can see? Does that annoy you?'

'I ask the questions, Roman! You just stick to answers.'

During the silence that followed, McDermott glared daggers at Roman. Eventually he said, 'I'll be back in a moment,' as he stepped swiftly through the door, locking it as he went.

Roman knew that it would be more than a moment. He was right. It was a little over half an hour. By then he was starting to get angry.

'Let's start back at the beginning,' McDermott said as he re-entered the room.

'If Detective Marsh is not available, then I'd like to speak to another senior officer, Mr McDermott.'

'Don't get on your high horse with me, Roman!'

'Am I being charged?'

'Not yet.'

'Am I being held in custody?'

A glare was the only response from McDermott.

'Then I take it I can leave at any time I wish?'

'When I've finished with you, and not before!'

'Why is another officer not present at this interview? Why is it not being recorded?'

'Don't you come the bush lawyer with me!'

'And that's another point. If I'm not allowed to leave, then I'd like my lawyer present, please.'

'Come off the grass!'

'I am here as a witness, not a suspect. I haven't been charged, and I wasn't booked in through the custody officer. If I leave now, Mr McDermott—immediately—I'm prepared to forget about this. If you attempt any further delay, there will be a stink, and most of the smell will attach to you.'

For a minute and a half there was a battle of wills, as Roman and McDermott stared, unblinking, at each other. Then it was over.

'I haven't finished with you, Roman,' said the detective as he held the door open, 'I'll find a way to charge you with something. "Obstructing police in the course of their duty" might cover it. Don't think you've won. I'll get you yet.'

A minute later Roman was standing on the footpath in Archer Street, drinking in the midday sunshine, and putting the vitriol of one small-minded policeman behind him.

He ate a salad sandwich as he walked through the Westfield shopping complex, thinking and planning as he walked. He didn't underrate McDermott, and the best way to prevent any trouble from that quarter would be to solve the murder—as quickly as possible! Back to the investigation then, decided Roman. And, since Jeff's guilt originated somewhere in his past, it was time to go back to Ramsgate.

According to the note from Greg Ottway, Jeff's first employers were a company called A. G. Bright & Sons. The phone book gave an address in Sans Souci.

When Roman pulled up in front he found it to be an old, brick building with an open roller door revealing a large workshop. Through the glass panels of the adjacent door Roman could see a mousy secretary typing at an untidy desk. He pushed open the door and stepped into the office.

'Good afternoo . . .' she started to say, and then changed it to, 'Good heavens! Are you Mark Roman?'

'I'm afraid I am,' he said with a smile. 'Guilty as charged.'

'Oh . . . oh . . .' she said, 'what can we do for you, Mr Roman?'

'I'd like to speak to the boss, if I may?'

'Yes . . . yes . . . of course. Young Mr Bright, or Old Mr Bright?'

'Old Mr Bright, I think.'

'Straightaway, Mr Roman,' she said, rising from her desk and hurrying through a rear door.

A few moments later she returned with an elderly man wearing grey overalls that looked even older than he did.

'Mr Bright, this is Mark Roman,' said the secretary brightly. 'Mr Roman—Mr Arthur Bright.'

'What can I do for you, Mr Roman?' asked the old man suspiciously.

'I'm looking into the death of Jeff Ottway.'

'Oh, I see.'

'With the encouragement of Greg and Beryl Ottway, I might add. I got to know Jeff in the last few days of his life, you see.'

'You'd better step into my office,' said Bright, turning around and leading the way through the rear door. This led into the high-roofed workshop, where several young men in overalls stopped what they were doing and stared at the visitor.

'Get back to work, you lot!' snapped the old man. 'He's here to see me, not you.'

In the far corner was a glassed-in office. Inside, Bright gestured for Roman to take a seat.

'Now, what can I do for you?' he asked, as he lowered himself into a battered leather chair behind a desk piled high with scraps of paper.

'Jeff Ottway did his apprenticeship here, I believe?'

'Yes, he did. He's on the wall.'

As he spoke, the old man spun the chair around and gestured at a cork-board covering the wall behind him. The board was packed with photographs. Ancient, fading black-and-white snaps jostled with newer colour photos.

'He's here somewhere,' said Bright, rising from his chair, 'Let me see. Ah . . . yes . . . here he is.'

He detached a photograph from the board and handed it to Roman. It was a group shot of three young men in overalls. Despite the fact that the picture must have been taken over twelve years ago and was starting to curl with age, Roman could identify Jeff in the group.

'He's the one in the middle?' asked Roman.

'That's right.'

'And who are the other two?'

'This one,' said Bright, stabbing at the photo with a nicotine-stained forefinger, 'is David Stacey.'

Roman looked closely at the short, skinny kid on Ottway's right.

'And the other is Peter O'Neil.'

Arthur Bright leaned back and let out a long sigh.

'Within six months of that picture being taken,' he said, 'Peter was dead, David was crippled, and Jeff had quit. I lost three of my best boys in six months.'

136

CHAPTER 9

'Tell me about it,' said Roman.

'There's nothing to tell,' replied Arthur, with a shrug of his shoulders. 'It was just one of those runs of bad luck that happen occasionally. Peter was a keen rock fisherman. He was caught by a freak wave early one Sunday morning. His body was washed up on the beach three days later.'

'And David?'

'Knocked down by a hit-and-run driver. In hospital for three months. Lost the use of his legs permanently. No good in the electrical trade.'

'And Jeff?'

'I don't know,' Arthur hesitated, 'I think he just got depressed over what had happened to his two best mates. Anyway, he left. Got a job on the North Shore somewhere. I was sorry to lose him. Jeff Ottway was a good worker and a polite kid. Not like the kids today.'

Roman looked at the photograph again: Peter O'Neil, looking broad-shouldered, solid and sensible (but not sensible enough, when it came to rock fishing!); David Stacey, a whole head shorter than Jeff and as thin as a rake; and Jeff Ottway, looking remarkably like the man Roman had met more than ten years later.

'I wonder if you could help me get in touch with . . .' began Roman.

137

'I probably can,' interrupted Arthur Bright, 'I'm a bit of a magpie, Mr Roman, I hoard things. Hang on.'

With that he began opening desk drawers and hunting through scraps of paper that looked like nothing less than a complete mess to Roman, but which apparently meant something to Bright.

'David Stacey's father is dead, but I know that his mother is in a nursing home somewhere. I know I wrote it down,' he muttered as he searched.

'What about David Stacey himself?'

'No idea. Ah! Here it is. David's mum, Iris Stacey, is in a Maroubra Junction nursing home. I'll copy out the address for you.'

He did this and passed over a scrap of notepaper.

'What about Peter O'Neil?' Roman asked.

'You could try a seance.'

'Any family? That's what I meant!'

'His parents are both dead, I think. But I seem to remember a sister. Now what was her married name? She used to live at Kurnell, I think. And she married a bloke named . . . Plumber! That was it. He wasn't, though.'

'Wasn't what?'

'Wasn't a plumber. Plumber was just his name. I think he was a carpet layer. Or maybe a carpet salesman,' Arthur continued, his brow furrowed at the effort of concentration. 'If she still lives there, you might find her in the phone book. It's on that pile behind you, Mr Roman.'

Roman turned around, found the L–Z section of the White Pages, and turned to the Ps. There were only three entries with the surname Plumber—and only one of them was in Kurnell.

'May I use your phone?'

'Here it is,' said Arthur, pushing across the desk a phone that had once been ivory but was now smudged with greasy thumb and finger marks.

'You don't happen to remember her Christian name?' asked Roman as he dialled.

'As a matter of fact, I do. I ended up seeing quite a bit of her when Peter died. Their parents were already dead, so I helped her sort out the estate. It's Laurel.'

Just then the ringing phone was answered.

'Hello?'

'Laurel Plumber?'

'Yes.'

'My name is Mark Roman. I wonder if I could talk to you about an old friend of your late brother's—Jeff Ottway.'

'Jeff? What do you want to know?'

'Could I call around and see you?'

'I guess so. If you want to. But I haven't seen Jeff for ten years or more.'

He promised her he'd be there in half an hour, and hung up.

'Thanks for all your help, Arthur,' said Roman, shaking the old man's hand.

'Just so long as you catch the bastard that killed poor Jeff. He was a top bloke.'

Roman left Sans Souci by Rocky Point Road. He crossed the Captain Cook Bridge over the Georges River, and turned into Captain Cook Drive. He found the house not far from Cronulla High School, with a view from its front verandah across Woolooware Bay.

Laurel Plumber looked harried. She had bleached, dish-mop hair, and anxious, blue eyes.

'It was only after I got off the phone,' she said,

139

standing back and holding the door open, 'that I realised it was *the* Mark Roman I was talking to. Sorry I didn't recognise your voice at once.'

'Don't be silly, that's nothing to be sorry about.'

'Tea? Coffee?'

'I wouldn't say no to a cup of tea. White with two sugars, please.'

Over the tea he explained the nature of his mission.

'I'm sorry about Jeff,' said Laurel, 'but I'd be very surprised if I could help in any way.'

'Jeff's guilt problem that I told you about seems to go back to his past. Probably back to when he was living in this area. Perhaps from around the time of his marriage.'

'I was there for the wedding,' said Laurel. 'Lesley made a lovely bride. But there wasn't anything wrong. I mean nothing for Jeff to be guilty about.'

'How long before the wedding did your brother die?'

'About four months. Or four and a half months. Something like that.'

'I hope I'm not reviving painful memories?' Roman murmured sympathetically.

'It's been a long time,' shrugged the young woman philosophically, 'the scars have healed.'

'How close were Jeff and Peter?'

'Very close. Peter, Jeff and David were best mates. Hung around together all the time.'

'That's David Stacey?'

'That's right.'

'You wouldn't happen to know where he is these days, would you?'

'Not any more. For a long time he lived in his

140

family home, even after his mum went into the nursing home. But he sold that and moved out a few months ago. I remember seeing the house on the display board of a real estate place in Rockdale at least three months ago.'

'Did Jeff Ottway ever go rock fishing with Peter?'

'Sometimes. But Peter was the real fanatic. He'd get up at the crack of dawn, even in winter, to go fishing.'

'Is there any possibility that Jeff might have blamed himself for Peter's death?'

'I don't see how,' said Laurel, looking puzzled.

'Maybe Jeff was supposed to go with Peter that morning, and failed to turn up, and thought that if he'd been there he could have saved your brother.'

'But he *was* there!'

'Was he? I didn't know that.'

'It was Jeff and Peter, just the two of them, who were out on the rocks that day. It was Jeff who raised the alarm.'

'What exactly happened to Peter?'

'What happens to a lot of rock fishermen, sadly. They were fishing off the rocks at Inscription Point—on the southern headland of Botany Bay. They'd often fished there before, and they were both confident that they knew what they were doing. Anyway, Peter was just too close to the edge when there was a freak wave that washed him off the rocks and sucked him under.'

'Did you talk to Jeff about it much afterwards?'

'Not much. Just enough so that I could understand, that's all. After that, I didn't really feel like talking about it at all.'

'What did Jeff tell you?'

141

'What I've just said. It was windy, and there was a strong swell running. Jeff was standing well north of Peter, almost on the corner of the headland. Peter was fifty yards away from Jeff, facing the open Pacific, when the wave struck. Jeff dropped his gear and ran over when he heard the scream. But by the time he got there, there was no trace of Peter.'

Even after a decade, moisture began to form in Laurel's eyes as she told the story.

'Was there an inquest?' asked Roman gently.

'Yes,' she replied as she pulled out a crumpled tissue and wiped her nose.

'What was the verdict?'

'Death by misadventure. A funny way to put it, I always thought. Peter knew the risks. The risks were part of it. Standing on wet rocks, just a few yards away from a pounding sea—he loved that. It was the adventure that killed him—not "misadventure," whatever that means.'

'Did Jeff ever say that he could have prevented it? Or should have prevented it?'

'Just once. On the day it happened. He kept saying: "If only I'd been closer." But after he'd been back to the spot with a police sergeant from Cronulla he didn't say it again. The sergeant pointed out that these things happen quickly. Only wearing a life jacket would have saved Peter. Jeff accepted that.'

'And Peter didn't bother with a life jacket?'

'He laughed at the idea. He said only girls wore life jackets—real blokes didn't.'

Laurel twisted her hands together, and bit on her lip. Roman let the silence hang in the room.

'It was Peter's fault,' she said at last. 'Peter was

142

careless, and that's why Peter died. I didn't like to face it at the time, but I can face it now.'

'Did *you* ever blame Jeff? Did you ever tell him it was his fault?'

'No!' Laurel was genuinely shocked by the suggestion. 'Jeff was our friend. We went to high school together. All of us. Jeff, Lesley, Peter, David, me—a whole bunch of us. And Jeff was one of the nicest boys in the bunch. I could never have said anything like that to him.'

Later, as he drove up The Grand Parade, around the rim of Botany Bay, Roman thought about what she had said. Could Peter's death not have been an accident? Had Jeff and Peter quarrelled, had Jeff pushed Peter into the turbulent sea? Was Jeff Ottway a murderer?

That would certainly explain the heavy burden of guilt he talked about. But did it fit with the other parts of his story? He had talked about apologising to his 'victim': clearly not Peter O'Neil. Who then? Laurel? If so, why hadn't she said something about it to Roman? On top of which, she didn't strike Roman as harbouring a 'vicious' hatred of Jeff Ottway. Quite the opposite, in fact, if she was being as truthful as she appeared to be.

A loud blast on a truck horn made Roman drag his attention away from the murder of Jeff Ottway and back to his surroundings. On his right, Botany Bay was sparkling in the autumn sunshine. On his left was an eclectic mixture of new houses, renovated old houses and blocks of units, all designed to take advantage of the views across the bay to the distant Pacific horizon. Roman liked his leafy North Shore, but he harboured a small fantasy

143

about living in a place like this—with wide views and a salty tang in the breeze.

His fantasy spoiled as he negotiated the traffic around him. The Grand Parade was six lanes of non-stop noise and carbon monoxide. Looking at the bay through plate glass would be fine—as long as you didn't open the window to let in the exhaust and the traffic's roar. Still musing, Roman drove past the airport, turned right, and before long was passing the disused Bunnerong Power Station. He turned into Bunnerong Road and then into Fitzgerald Avenue. There he almost got himself lost, but just as he was about to pull over and check the Gregory's, he passed a street sign and discovered that he was in Maroubra Road—exactly where he wanted to be!

The nursing home was an impressive three-storey building. Roman parked in a side-street, and made his way to the reception desk.

'Iris Stacey? That was the name?' said the smartly dressed young woman at reception.

'That's right.'

'And your name is . . . ?'

'Mark Roman.'

'Oh, yes! Of course! I was wondering why I recognised the voice. Are you a friend of the family, Mr Roman?'

'A distant friend,' lied Roman, shuffling his feet uncomfortably, and stuffing his hands deeper into his pockets.

'It's just that David Stacey never mentioned you. And with a friend who is a celebrity . . . well . . .'

She left the unasked question hanging, and Roman made no attempt to answer it.

'Second floor—room 213, Mr Roman,' said the

receptionist after she had checked her computer screen. 'You can go up now, if you wish.'

Roman followed the directions up a broad flight of stairs. The door to room 213 stood open, and the bed inside was empty. But across the room was a door that opened onto a sunny, glassed-in balcony. On the balcony was a grey-haired lady in a rocking chair.

'Mrs Stacey?'

She turned and looked at him with vacant eyes.

She said nothing, so Roman sat down on a footstool, to bring his eyes down to her level. She was staring at him now, suspiciously.

'My name is Mark Roman, Mrs Stacey. And I was wondering if you could help me.'

She still said nothing.

'Would you answer a few questions for me?'

Iris Stacey's jaw moved as if she was chewing on something, but she said nothing.

'It's about an old friend of your son David—Jeff Ottway. Do you remember Jeff Ottway, Mrs Stacey?'

'I know you,' said Iris Stacey slowly, in a voice that crackled with age, 'you're on the wireless.'

'That's right,' Roman responded, speaking slowly himself, 'At night.'

'Hmmm. At night. On the wireless at night.'

There was a silence, and Roman thought it best to let this information sink in before continuing.

'At night,' said Iris Stacey again, 'I listen.'

'Good,' said Roman warmly, 'I'm glad you listen. It's always good to meet a listener.'

'You're nice,' said Iris, with a sudden smile, 'not like that Jack Kingston. He's rude!'

'Jack's actually a nice man. It's just the style in which he does his show.'

'He's rude!' insisted Iris. 'But you're nice.'

She turned and looked out of the big, plate-glass window for a moment, then she turned back and asked, 'Do you know David?'

'No, I'm afraid I don't know your son, Mrs Stacey. But I did know a friend of his—Jeff Ottway. Do you remember Jeff Ottway?'

'You should tell him to come more often.'

'Jeff Ottway?'

'My son. David doesn't come and visit me often enough.'

'If I meet him, I'll tell him,' promised Roman. 'Do you remember David's friend—Jeff Ottway?'

'Jeff . . . ?'

'Jeff Ottway,' Roman prompted.

'I remember young Jeffrey,' said Iris brightly, after a long pause. 'He married that little girl with the honey blonde hair. What was her name? Was it . . . Lesley?'

'Yes, that's right, Mrs Stacey. Jeff Ottway married Lesley. Although I'm afraid they're divorced now.'

'Divorced? Ah, they all get divorced these days. Not like in my day. "For richer for poorer, in sickness and in health, until death us do part," we said. And we meant it, too.'

'Did David ever talk to you much about Jeff?'

'Divorced? That's very sad really. Common. But sad.'

'Yes, it is.'

'David and Jeff were best friends. When they were school boys in short pants. Best mates, they were.'

146

'Did they remain friends as they grew older?'

'Friends? Yes! Of course they did. Best friends. My David idolised Jeff. Wanted to be just like him. If you ask me, David was at least half in love with Lesley too. That's why he was in such a bad mood at their wedding. Jealousy.'

'They worked together, didn't they?'

'Worked?'

'David and Jeff—they worked together as electricians, didn't they?'

'David followed in Jeff's footsteps. He idolised him, you know.'

Quite abruptly Iris Stacey stopped talking, and her eyes looked into the distance in an unfocused away, as if she was seeing, not the scenery, but the past. For some moments she sat and stared, breathing heavily.

Roman was about to ask if she was alright, when she suddenly spoke again.

'David was so pleased. As pleased as Punch. Tickled pink he was, when he got an apprenticeship in the same firm as Jeff.'

'Did David ever have a falling out with Jeff?'

'A falling out?'

'An argument of any sort?'

'Oh, I suppose so. Everyone argues sometimes. Even the best of friends.'

'What did they argue about? Why did they fall out?'

'Oh, I don't know that, dear. I listen, you know. Every night on the wireless. You're very nice to your callers. That's why I like you.'

'That's very kind of you to say that. Does David ever talk about Jeff these days?'

'These days? No. Not these days. He doesn't

visit me often enough. When you see David, tell him to come more often.'

'If I see him, I'll do that. Tell me about David's accident, Mrs Stacey.'

Alarmingly, a large tear began to form in the corner of one eye when Roman asked this question.

'Poor David,' said Iris, with a throb in her voice. 'Poor little David.'

'I'm sorry I asked, Mrs Stacey. Don't talk about it, if it distresses you.'

'Poor, poor David. He was never strong, you know, never a big boy. Always thin and weedy, all through his childhood. And when that car hit him, it would have bounced him around like a leaf. That's what the doctors told us at the time. He had been bounced around like a leaf.'

Roman waited for her to say more. He was reluctant to prompt, for fear of distressing her or having some effect on her health. After a long moment, she spoke again.

'It was a Saturday morning. I remember it well. A policeman knocked on our door. "I'm afraid I have bad news for you," said the policeman, "about your son." And we both thought he was dead. We talked about it afterwards, Ted and I, and the same thought had sprung into both our minds at the same instant: that David was dead. It was such a relief to hear that he was alive. No matter how bad the injuries were, we were just glad that he was alive.'

'Did they tell you how the accident happened?'

'Hit-and-run, it was. The car that hit David came around a corner behind him. David never saw the car or the driver. It came around a corner. Behind him. Very fast. And then it didn't stop. The driver just left David lying in the road. Left him for dead. It was a milkman who found him.'

'A milkman? So it was early in the morning, was it?'

'Yes. Didn't you know? It was only just sunrise when the accident happened.'

'What was David doing out that early in the morning?'

'Jogging. Even in winter he went jogging very early in the morning. Trying to build himself up, trying to be more like his hero, Jeff Ottway.'

Iris Stacey began to breathe heavily again. Then her breathing settled down, and she turned to Roman, looked him straight in the eyes, and spoke very earnestly.

'It was wicked. That's what it was. Wicked. To knock down a young man in the prime of life. And not even stop the car.'

'Yes. You're quite right.'

'He always went jogging,' said Iris brightly, as if her mind had skipped onto another track. 'He was wearing his green tracksuit on the day of the accident. His green one. I remember. The police-man drove us to hospital. I never saw that tracksuit again. They had to cut it off him, they said. He was in emergency surgery when we got to the hospital. And we sat for hours, in that room smell-ing of carbolic. Waiting and waiting. When they let us see him, he was in intensive care. He was stable, they said. There was no brain damage. The prognosis was good.'

'Was he in the hospital for long?'

'I . . . I can't remember,' stumbled Iris, as though the flood of memories had suddenly hit a log-jam. 'It must have been a long time, mustn't it? And then there was rehabilitation afterwards. That went on for a long time. Poor David.'

'How has David coped since?'

Iris appeared not to hear the question. She rested her head back against the chair-back and stared into the distance.

'How has David coped since the accident?' Roman repeated.

'David?'

'Your son—David. How has he coped since the accident?'

'He's a good boy. But he should come more often. You tell him to come more often.'

'Yes. Yes, of course,' murmured Roman with a sigh.

'I listen every night. You're very nice.'

Later, back in his car, Roman's mind was buzzing with all he had learned in the course of the afternoon. He thought of the tragedies in Jeff Ottway's past. Had Jeff felt guilt about what had happened to his best friends? Did he blame himself?

And then there was Craig Connors. What was Connors hiding? Why was he so aggressive and tight-lipped at the pub? Had he really hated Jeff Ottway? And, if so, did it have anything to do with Jeff's murder?

These thoughts still occupied Roman's mind as the vast, steel canopy of the Sydney Harbour Bridge swept overhead. He was still mulling over these questions, turning them over and over in his mind, when he realised that he was almost in Chatswood, and heading towards Cambridge Street. The block of units in which Jeff Ottway was murdered kept drawing him back, like a magnet.

He parked his old green Volvo several doors down from the block of units, and slowly walked towards them. Roman felt as if he were projecting his thoughts ahead of himself, willing his thoughts to enter the building, to *understand* the lives of those who lived there: especially the lives of Jeff, Caitlin and Eleanor Ottway.

The late afternoon sun cast Roman's tall, broad-shouldered frame as a long, black shadow across the path that led to the building's entrance. This time, instead of going inside, Roman began to walk around the perimeter of the property. In his mind he pictured the electrician arriving home from work, greeted by his wife and child, eating an evening meal, sleeping with Caitlin—and then waking up in a cold sweat, haunted by a guilty nightmare. What sort of guilt lasts over a decade? Roman asked himself.

He reached the far side of the property, and stood opposite the Ottway unit. Inside, the lights were turned on and through the glass door he could see Caitlin talking to a young uniformed policeman. Some additional inquiries being made, Roman surmised—routine inquiries, otherwise Marsh or McDermott would have come in person.

Then the policeman held out his arms, and Caitlin rushed into them! They hugged each other warmly, then Caitlin buried her head in his chest as if smothering tears. Roman stared in bewilderment. What kind of relationship was he seeing?

Suddenly he felt grubby, like a peeping Tom, turned on his heels and walked quickly back towards the street. For some minutes he stood irresolutely on the footpath, unsure of what to do. Before he had reached a decision the policeman walked out of the building. He paid no attention to Roman, straddled a police motorbike, strapped a helmet on his head, and roared off up the street.

Roman trod heavily and reluctantly to the entrance and pressed the buzzer.

'Yes?'

'Caitlin, it's me, Mark Roman.'

'I'll let you in,' she said, without hesitation. Would she have hesitated a few minutes before? Roman wondered. Would she even have answered the buzzer?

The security door clicked loudly, Roman pushed, and it swung open. He strode in his heavy, flat-footed way down the carpeted corridor and knocked on the front door of the Ottways' unit.

Caitlin opened it almost immediately.

'Come in, Mark,' she said. Roman noticed that she looked flushed and pretty.

'Drink?'

'No thanks.'

'You're as bad as Jeff.'

'In what sense?'

'Jeff was almost teetotal. He had the occasional port after a meal in a restaurant, and that was about all. Maybe a light beer at a barbecue—but only one.'

'How very un-Australian,' said Roman lightly.

'I used to say the same thing, and joke with him about it,' replied Caitlin, the smile disappearing from her face. Quickly she pulled a handkerchief from her pocket and wiped her nose. The grief appeared genuine. Could she have a lover, and still feel genuine grief?

152

'How is your inquiry going?' she asked.

'I feel,' said Roman, 'I feel that I am drawing closer to understanding, closer to seeing the solution. But you must understand that it's a feeling, not a reasoning process.'

'I see. Or I think I do. So what have you found out today?'

'More about Jeff's early life, before you met him.'

'Useful?'

'Very.'

'But that's not why you came back tonight, is it?'

'No, it isn't,' Roman admitted.

'If you have more questions—ask them,' said Caitlin with a deep, weary sigh, running her fingers through her hair.

'Firstly, a very impolite question. But please let me ask it without becoming angry.'

'That depends on what it is,' Caitlin replied cautiously.

'Did Jeff have a lover?'

'No!'

'You're certain?'

'I would have known. I'm sure I would have known. And it would be so out of character. Jeff lived for me and Eleanor. He was a home-maker, not a playboy. We were saving up a deposit for a house of our own—a real house. Jeff wanted a yard and a shed. I have more confidence in Jeff's faithfulness than I can ever explain.'

Roman silently took all this in. Could she be so calm about a suggestion of Jeff's infidelity, if she had a lover herself?

'Secondly, you used to work at Comtel, didn't you?'

'That's right. That's where Jeff and I met.'

'Did you know a man named Craig Connors when you worked there?'

'Ah. So you've heard about that, have you?'

'Actually—I've heard nothing,' Roman said honestly.

'Then let me be the one to explain it to you—and put it into its proper context.' She took a deep breath, and then continued, 'Craig was my boyfriend. Years ago. Before Jeff came to Comtel. Soon after Jeff arrived, I dropped Craig and took up with Jeff. Craig was pretty upset for a while, but he got over it. End of story.'

'Why did you switch from Craig to Jeff?'

'I could say all the romantic things about human chemistry and sexual electricity and so on. And they'd all be true. But more mundane things came into it too. Jeff's better looking than Craig. And he has nicer manners. He's just a nicer, gentler man.'

Roman noticed that she still talked about Jeff in the present tense. Perhaps the full force of her husband's death was yet to hit her.

'You say that Craig Connors "got over it"—but are you sure?'

'What do you mean?'

'Could he have harboured a grudge against Jeff?'

'Over all this time? Surely not! Whatever makes you think that?'

'An anonymous message, phoned through to the radio station.'

'Saying . . . ?'

'Saying: "Find out why Craig Connors hated Jeff

Ottway." Now I know why he hated Jeff. Or, I know at least one reason. Perhaps there were more.'

'If so,' Caitlin said firmly, 'Jeff didn't know about it. He would have told me if he was having trouble with Craig.'

'Would he? Ex-boyfriend and all?'

'No. You've got it wrong, Mark. I went out with Craig for over a year. I know him. There is no way that Craig Connors could have murdered Jeff.'

But someone did, thought Roman, as he drove towards his radio station that night, someone did. Someone hated Jeff Ottway enough to creep up behind him, lift a spanner or tyre lever high above his head, and bring it down in a crushing blow. Someone hated him enough to do that. But who?

That night on his radio show he decided to do another light-weight topic rather than get back into the heavy stuff again. He chose 'Quotable Quotes', and from the beginning it worked like a dream.

Listeners rang to rattle off their favourites lines from P. G. Wodehouse ('She was one of those ice-cold secretaries only Genghis Khan would have dared to cross, and he only on one of his better days'), R.G. Menzies ('What's your policy on abortion, Mr Menzies?' 'In your case, sir, I'd make it retrospective'), and Winston Churchill ('Mr Churchill, you are drunk!' 'True, madam, but you are ugly; and in the morning I shall be sober').

But he still didn't escape the subject of forgiveness. 'Vivian of Bronte' rang to share a quote she had clipped from the bottom of a calender.

'Let's hear it,' said Mark.

'It says that someone named General Oglethorpe once remarked to John Wesley: "I never forgive", to which Wesley replied: "Then I hope, sir, that you never sin." Do you like that, Mark?'

'I like it very much. It sums up what I've been trying to get across earlier this week on the show when I've talked about forgiveness. Unless we both experience and offer forgiveness, we are in dead trouble, all of us.'

CHAPTER 10

Roman began the next day with his usual Saturday morning routine of supermarket shopping, and then set off for Lane Cove golf course to play a quick nine holes with Jack Kingston.

'You ignored my advice, didn't you?' said Kingston, as they walked onto the second tee.

'About . . . ?' prompted Roman.

'About getting involved,' Kingston replied, a note of irritation in his voice.

'Sorry, Jack. Call it weakness on my part, if you wish . . .'

'Call it lunacy, more likely!'

'I am only trying to help.'

'Leave help to the professionals,' Kingston muttered, as he lined up the club and steadied his feet to make his shot.

Roman waited until Kingston's ball was sailing high and straight down the middle of the fairway, and then asked, 'Could you have said "No," Jack?'

'Was there really a question?'

'What do you mean?'

'Are you responding to a cry for help, or your own curiosity?'

'Well . . .'

'I think I've made my point.'

'You're being a bit unfair,' murmured Roman, as he balanced the ball on the tee.

'You're standing too close to the ball,' Kingston said, as Roman took his stance. 'Shift your feet, Mark my lad, or you'll still be standing too close to the ball after you've hit it.'

Roman shifted his feet and made his shot. The ball came to rest beyond Kingston's but well to the left.

'You heard about the Texas oil man who bought his son a set of golf clubs, didn't you?' said Kingston, as they set off down the fairway. 'The boy gave one of the clubs away—it didn't have a swimming pool!'

'Talking about your joke book, how did your lunch with the publisher go?'

'Very well. I've left the manuscript with him. Tell me, Mark, has this latest foray of yours into murder and mystery brought you any grief yet?'

'Only with the police,' Roman muttered bitterly, thinking of Detective Constable McDermott.

'Only! And you still haven't learned your lesson?' said Kingston with a laugh. 'I'll see you on the green.'

'And I'll see this case to the bitter end,' Roman thought to himself.

In that mood of grim determination, after lunch he drove once more to Cambridge Street. Once more he pressed the button marked 'Neely.'

He waited for a minute, then pressed it again. And then a third time.

'Saturday afternoon,' he thought. 'They must be out.'

He was about to press Caitlin Ottway's buzzer, but something made him hesitate. After a moment's consideration his index finger hit the security buzzer with the name 'Shumack' under-neath.

'Yes?' grated the thin, metallic voice out of the intercom box.

'It's Mark Roman, Dylan. Would you let me in please?'

'Sure thing.'

Roman's plans were to try talking to those people on the first floor he had missed last time. But since Dylan Shumack had let him in, he felt an obligation to chat to him first. With this in mind, Roman knocked on Shumack's door. It opened instantly.

'Come in, Mark,' said the chubby young man as he spun around and led the way down the short hall.

'Did you know it was me?' he asked over his shoulder.

'You? When?' Roman replied.

'On the air. On your show. The other night.'

'Oh, then. Yes, I recognised the name. And I recognised your voice as well.'

'Did you?' asked Shumack. 'Recognise my voice, I mean?'

'Yes. But that's something I find easy to do. Maybe it comes from working in radio for so many years. I just seem to be tuned into voices.'

Shumack raked some comic books off a chair and said, 'Sit down. Would you like a Coke?'

Roman didn't feel much like a Coke, but he didn't have the heart to reject the young man's enthusiastic attempt at hospitality.

'Sure,' he replied.

'How about a Mars Bar as well? I've got a whole box of them in the fridge.'

'Just a Coke—that'll be fine,' said Roman hur-riedly.

159

A moment later Shumack came wheeling back around the corner from the tiny kitchenette and skidded to a halt, leaving a black, rubber tyre mark on the tiles.

'I nearly got that stupid old bat's little dog,' he said with a laugh, as he threw a can of Coke over to Roman and opened one for himself.

'Which dog?'

'The Neely dame next door has got this really wussy little dog.'

'Yes, I know the one you mean.'

'Well, I nearly skittled it the other day,' said the young man with an unpleasant laugh, and then paused to take a swig from his can. Roman didn't reply.

'The old bat left it running around in the lobby while she went to the footpath to collect the mail. I aimed my wheels at the little mongrel and took off at top speed. The over-grown rat saw me coming and took evasive action. I nearly got it, though. I came *that* close,' chortled Shumack, holding up two fingers an inch apart.

Roman drank his Coke in silence.

'It was great talking to you on the air, Mark,' he continued, unaware of how his guest had reacted to his story. 'Can I call again some time?'

'Sure. Any time,' murmured Roman, 'whenever you have anything worth sharing. You have to get past my producer. But you can do that just by persuading him that you've got something worth saying on the air.'

'Okay—I'll do that. Why are you back here today? Still investigating?'

'Yes, still investigating. I thought I'd try to catch those residents on the first floor I missed last time.

160

See if they heard or saw anything on the night Jeff died.'

'Worth a try, I guess.'

Roman took this as a cue to escape, thanked the young man for his hospitality, and let himself out.

The two apartments on the first floor he had not yet visited were occupied, so he'd been told, by a woman named April Myers and a merchant banker named Morgan Simmonds. He didn't know which door was which, so he chose a door at random and knocked.

The knock was not answered immediately, but he could hear a radio playing inside, so Roman knocked again. In response, a middle-aged woman opened the door. She was wearing a floral dress and fluffy slippers. As the door swung open the sound of the radio became clearer: it was playing what Roman called 'lift music'—schmaltzy strings playing old romantic ballads.

'Ms April Myers?' asked Roman.

'*Miss*,' she replied firmly, 'I am *Miss* April Myers. And who are you?'

'My name is Mark Roman.'

She squinted at him, like someone who should be wearing glasses but wasn't.

'So you are,' she agreed, 'so you are. You're the one who discovered that poor young man's body downstairs earlier this week.'

'That's right,' said Roman, putting as much warmth into his resonant voice as he possibly could, 'and with the support of his widow, I'm asking residents of this block if they saw or heard anything on the night Jeff died. I wonder if I might step in for a moment and ask you a few questions?'

'No! You may not! I do not allow men inside my apartment. Ask your questions here.'

'Oh. Alright, then,' Roman said, a little put out by the vehemence of her reply. 'Jeff was killed in the early hours of Tuesday morning—between midnight and one a.m. Were you home? Did you hear anything at that time—anything at all?'

'I used to listen to your radio program,' said April Myers, ignoring his question, 'but I stopped. I can't remember now why I stopped. But something upset me.'

'The night Jeff Ottway died, Miss Myers . . .' prompted Roman.

'Ah, yes. I don't think I did hear anything. Nothing special, that is. I always hear things in the night. I'm not a very good sleeper. Sometimes I wake up at three or four in the morning. Just wide awake. And I have to listen to the radio, or turn on my light and read for an hour or more before I can get back to sleep.'

'Tuesday morning—or Monday night, if you prefer to think of it that way, Miss Myers: were you awake then?'

'Monday? Or early Tuesday? I'm not sure.'

'Anything you remember might help.'

'Now, why did I stop listening to your radio show? There was a reason, I know. I just can't recall what the reason was.'

'The time when Jeff Ottway died,' persisted Roman, 'were you awake? Were there any sounds at all?'

'There are always sounds! I've told you that!' April Myers snapped. 'Quite often it's the trains.'

'The trains?'

'The railway is not very far away. Just over in

162

that direction,' she gestured as she spoke. 'And the goods trains come through at the most unearthly hours. They always wake me up.'

'Did anything wake you between midnight and one a.m. on Tuesday morning?'

'What kind of "anything"? You mean the sound of someone being murdered? If I'd heard anything like that, I'd have told the police. Hold on, I think I've remembered . . .'

'Yes?' said Roman eagerly.

'I think I've remembered why I stopped listening to your show,' April Myers said triumphantly. 'It's come back to me now. It was because you talk about religion too much. You go on about Christianity.'

'Well, from time to time . . .' began Roman defensively.

'Now let me tell you something, Mr Roman,' continued Myers, her voice taking on an aggressive and angry tone. 'I was brought up in the church. My mother was priest-ridden all her life, poor woman. All that Christianity is about is *guilt*! That's all—just making people feel *guilty*!'

And with that, she slammed the door in his face.

'No, Christianity is all about . . .' Roman was saying as the door banged shut just a few inches in front of his nose, '. . . is all about forgiveness, not guilt,' he continued to the closed door, hoping that his voice would carry through to the other side.

As he turned to go he saw a young man fitting a key into the lock of the apartment door opposite.

'Morgan Simmonds?' Roman inquired.

'Yes? How can I help you?' he replied, turning around to face Roman.

He was wearing designer jeans and a striped, open-necked shirt. His blond hair was clipped short and brushed back, and he carried a black leather document case under his arm.

'My name is Mark Roman. I wonder if I could ask you a few questions.'

'What about?'

'About Jeff Ottway's murder.'

'Hold on—you're that radio chappie, the one who found the body?'

'That's right.'

'Come in, if you like. Ask me anything you like. But I won't be any help, I'm afraid.'

Simmonds led the way in, dropping his document case on a coffee table.

'Take a pew, Mr Roman. I'm about to make myself a cup of very strong coffee—will you join me?'

'Yes. Thank you very much,' Roman said, as he lowered his heavy frame into an armchair and took a look around. The apartment was expensively furnished in a stark, modern style.

From the kitchenette came the sound of coffee beans being ground, then of water boiling. A few minutes later Simmonds returned, carrying a coffee plunger and two cups.

'Do you need milk or sugar, Mr Roman?'

'Both, please.'

A moment later he returned with milk and sugar, pushed down the plunger, and then poured the coffee.

'Now I'm starting to feel human again,' Simmonds said as he sipped his coffee.

'You've worked on a Saturday?' Roman asked, gesturing to the document case on the table.

'It's still Friday in New York and the foreign exchange markets are open,' explained Simmonds. 'But that's not what you wanted to ask me about.'

'Quite right. Jeff Ottway called my radio show, and, as a result of that, I got to know him, and I was the one who found his body in the building on Tuesday morning.'

'I read about that in the newspaper. I'm afraid I'm not a listener to your show, Mr Roman. I'm too busy to listen to anything more than a ten-minute news bulletin.'

'There isn't a law. You don't have to listen to my show. But I am hoping that you might have heard something around the time when Jeff Ottway was killed.'

'And that was—when exactly?'

'Between midnight and one a.m., early on Tuesday morning.'

'Well, my girlfriend stayed with me that night. We were awake until about two, I think. But I can't recall hearing anything that sounded like murder.'

'I think Jeff was killed on the lawn outside his apartment. If that's so, then just possibly something was heard up here on the first floor.'

'I wish I could help, Mr Roman—but I don't recall anything.'

'Did you hear *anything*—anything at all, during the hour in question?'

'Oh, sure. There are always noises in an apartment building. But there was nothing unusual.'

'It doesn't matter whether it was unusual or not: what did you hear?'

'Well—as best I can recall—cars driving into the car park, I heard the lift a few times; that sort of thing. Maybe there was someone in the corridor on this floor at one stage. Although I'm not sure about that. On second thoughts, maybe that wasn't Tuesday. Sorry—there's not much there that can help you, I'm afraid.'

'That's alright, Mr Simmonds. What matters is that I ask. No stone unturned—that sort of thing.'

'Sure.'

Morgan Simmonds showed Roman to the door of his apartment, and as the door clicked closed behind him Roman started to think fast and furiously. Like pieces of a jigsaw puzzle things were starting to come together in his mind. Only starting, but he could almost glimpse a possible pattern. Shaking his head in frustration, he decided that while he was on the first floor he would call on the Palmers. A cheerful 'Just a moment' from within answered his knock. A minute later the door swung open to reveal Meg Palmer in her wheelchair.

'Oh, hello, Mark. It's nice to see you again. Come in.'

As she spun her wheelchair around to lead him down the short hallway Roman noticed that she was carrying a feather-duster, and had a damp cleaning cloth draped across the arm of the wheelchair.

'Are you any closer to knowing who killed Jeff Ottway?' she asked.

'Just possibly I am.'

'Sounds exciting. Tell me more.'

'I wish I could. But just for the moment I want to keep my own counsel.'

Meg Palmer raised a quizzical eyebrow at him, but asked no more questions. As he followed her into the lounge/dining room he found her husband

Jason on a step-ladder cleaning the large, sliding glass doors that led out to the small balcony.

'Oh, hello, Mark,' he said, 'I thought I heard your voice. Nice to see you again.'

'Hard at work, I see,' said Roman, as he took a seat on the sofa.

'It's Meg who works me so hard. She's a demon for keeping this place spotless.'

Roman glanced around and noticed that the place *was* spotless—not a mark, not a speck of dust.

'But your arrival gives me an excuse for a break,' added Jason, climbing down off the step ladder.

'Mark says he's getting close to a solution,' said Meg.

'Oh, yes? Anything you can tell us about?' queried Jason.

'Not just yet,' rumbled Roman. 'But let me ask you a question.'

'Fire away,' said Meg.

'Have you seen anything of Caitlin since the murder?'

'Heaps. She was up here for dinner last night,' Meg replied.

'And Meg's forever dropping in to see her downstairs,' added Jason.

'How is she coping?' Roman asked.

'She's coping,' said Meg, 'and that's about all. She's putting on a brave face much of the time, but the tears are not far below the surface.'

'There's one other thing,' Roman persisted. 'This is going to sound like an offensive question—but, believe me, I don't mean it that way. It's just that it's got to be asked if I'm to clear away the fog and see the truth.'

'Ask anything,' said a puzzled Meg.

'Could either Jeff or Caitlin have had a lover?' blurted out Roman.

'Impossible!' snorted Jason with a laugh. 'Out of the question. Ridiculous!'

Meg was quieter and more thoughtful, but her answer was the same: 'I can understand why you have to ask, Mark. But I'm sure Jason's right. Maybe we didn't know them well enough—but, I just can't see it. Not either of them. Not ever.'

Roman stayed with the Palmers for another ten minutes or so, just to be sociable. They were a nice young couple, he decided as they chatted, full of the sheer joy of life.

'Shall we tell him our news?' Meg asked Jason, just as Roman was rising to leave.

'It's a bit soon to start telling people,' Jason protested, 'we've only just found out ourselves.'

'But I *want* to tell people! Everyone!'

'Alright! Alright!,' Jason surrendered. 'The fact is, Mark . . .'

'That I'm pregnant!' interrupted Meg.

'Congratulations,' Roman responded. 'I'm delighted for both of you. How far gone are you?'

'Only six weeks!' said Jason with a mock groan, 'I'll have to put up with Meg's impatience for another seven and half months yet.'

'But it is so exciting, isn't it, Mark?' she burbled.

'Your first, obviously,' Roman said, smiling widely at their excitement and sheer pleasure.

'Yes, our first,' Meg answered. 'And I may not even need to have a Caesarian. We're not sure yet. Of course, in the end I may have. But quite possibly I'll get by without the Caesar. Isn't that great!'

For some minutes more Roman shared their enthusiasm. Then he shook hands with Jason, and kissed Meg on the cheek, and left them.

He had one last stop before leaving the building for the day—Caitlin Ottway.

Her apartment door was opened by a police constable. The same uniformed officer Roman had seen embracing Caitlin the night before!

'Oh, if I'm not intruding,' he stumbled, 'I've just called to see Caitlin for a moment.'

'No, you're not intruding,' said the policeman, 'Come in. I'm sure Caitlin would love to see you.'

The officer stood back and held the door open, and then followed Roman inside.

'Oh, hello, Mark,' said Caitlin, rising to her feet from the sofa. 'Thanks for dropping in again. Have you met my brother?' she added, gesturing towards the young policeman standing behind Roman's shoulder.

'Your brother?' Roman said.

'Yes. Mark, meet my little brother, Rod. Rod—Mark Roman.'

The two men shook hands.

'I . . . I assumed you were here on official business,' said Roman, to cover his embarrassment at misinterpreting the relationship.

'Entirely unofficial,' said the younger brother. 'Constable Rod Prior is the name. But I recognised you, of course, the minute I set eyes on you.'

'Take a seat, Mark,' said Caitlin.

'No, I won't stay. I just popped in to see how you're going.'

'I'm fine. It's not easy. But Rod's called in as often as he can. And Meg and Jason have been wonderful. Mum and Dad are flying up next Tuesday, and bringing Eleanor with them.'

'Has she been told?'

'Not yet,' Caitlin said, her voice dropping almost to a whisper, and moisture gleaming in her eyes. 'I said I wanted to be the one to explain to her.'

'Yes, of course, I understand,' Roman responded.

For a moment the atmosphere was heavy with loss. To break the silence the young policeman spoke, 'I must say, you're not the flavour of the month down at the station, just at the moment, Mark.'

'I got that message loud and clear yesterday,' said Roman sourly.

'Personally, I can't see what McDermott is beefing about. Of course, if a journalist gets caught up in a murder case that journalist is going to keep nosing around looking for a story.'

'There's a bit more to it than that, Rod,' Roman said defensively. 'I do feel a degree of responsibility. I was the one who encouraged Jeff to confront the person he had hurt all those years ago. If that really did play a role in the murder, well, I can't just let it go.'

'There's no need to explain, Mark,' said Caitlin, 'I understand. We all just need to know what happened. And why. The hurt won't be over for me until I understand.'

'I've been to see Jeff's parents,' Roman said, shifting the conversation onto safer ground.

'Yes, I know. Greg and Beryl have been on the phone to me every day. They've been very supportive.'

'And I've seen Jeff's first wife, and tracked

down some of his old friends—from before the time when you knew him.'

'And has it helped?' asked Caitlin.

'I think so. I . . .' Roman was about to say more, when he noticed Constable Rod Prior looking at him very closely, and decided that anything he said would be carried back to the police station—and it was too soon for that.

'Well, as long as you're okay,' said Roman, rising from his seat. 'Don't hesitate to get in touch if there's anything else I can do.'

That night Roman phoned out for a pizza and then, as he ate, he sat at his dining room table trying to fit together the pieces of the jigsaw puzzle of Jeff Ottway's life. He wrote the name of each person who played a role in the story on a small scrap of paper. Then he moved the scraps around, looking for ways they might connect, or for associations he had missed.

He went to bed that night feeling close to a solution, but unsure what that solution might be.

Sunday passed in a kind of haze. He put the car through the car-wash in the morning and went to church at night. Hugh Marsden preached a second sermon in his series on forgiveness. But all day Roman felt distracted, disconnected from reality. The pieces of the puzzle kept spinning around in his brain.

He was still in that state when he went to sleep.

Suddenly, he found himself wide awake again. He looked at his bedside clock: just after four a.m. Roman put his head back on the pillow and stared at the ceiling in the dark. As he did so, he was startled to discover that he knew the solution to the murder. While he had slept, his unconscious mind had re-shuffled the pieces into the correct order, and, the more he thought about it, the clearer it became. He knew, he *knew* for sure, who had killed Jeff Ottway—and how, and why.

He got out of bed and stumbled his way to the kitchen. As he made a hot milk drink he went over and over the facts in his mind. It all fitted together, but what should he do about it? Did he have enough evidence to take to the police? Would they even listen to him?

What should he do?

He took his drink to the table and began scribbling on a sheet of paper as he sipped. Yes, he thought, that's what I'll do. And I'll do it first thing in the morning.

Once that was settled, Roman went back to bed and slept like a baby.

In the morning he made himself patiently go through his regular morning routine. He walked up and bought a newspaper, and then did his basic preparation for Monday night's show. He didn't know how chaotic the rest of the day would be, and he wanted to be prepared in case he got no further chance to think about the show.

When he was satisfied that he had done all that he could, he got into his old green Volvo and drove, once again, to Cambridge Street, Chatswood.

Once more he pressed the 'Neely' button at the front security door.

'Hello? Who is it?'

'It's me, Jayne. Mark Roman. Will you let me in please.'

'Yes, of course. Just a moment.'

Shortly afterwards the front door clicked, and

Roman entered. Jayne Neely was waiting for him by her apartment door, nursing her poodle in her arms.

'Good morning, Mark!' she gushed. 'We're pleased to see our Mr Roman again, aren't we, Rachel?' she added, scratching the poodle's head. 'Come in and have some tea or coffee, Mark.'

'In a little while, Jayne,' Roman said. 'I want to see a neighbour of yours first. Is that okay?'

'I suppose so,' she muttered, and disappeared inside her apartment.

Roman walked to the door next to the Neelys' and knocked. A moment later it was opened by Dylan Shumack.

'Back again, Mark?' he said with delight. 'Come in. Come in. What can I do you for this time?'

'This time, Dylan,' said Mark, as he followed the chubby young man into the untidy unit, 'I want you to tell me something. I want you to tell me exactly how and why you murdered Jeff Ottway.'

CHAPTER 11

'You've gone bananas,' laughed Shumack. 'All that sitting in a soundproofed room talking to yourself has finally got to you.'

'I'm serious, Dylan,' said Roman.

'Well, I'm not taking you seriously,' snorted Shumack.

'But I know, Dylan,' said Roman, 'I really know.'

'There's nothing for you to know!'

'You won't tell me?'

'Yeah. Now you're starting to understand, mate, I won't discuss such a stupid idea.'

'In that case—*I'll* tell *you*,' said Roman in his deepest radio voice.

Shumack was abruptly quiet. His manner changed in an instant, as if it had suddenly dawned on him that this was serious.

Roman was seated in an armchair placed in front of a window. Against the light he looked huge and his shadow fell across the room, seeming to swallow up the chubby young man in the wheelchair.

'Alright. If you're so smart—tell me!' sneered Shumack, a note of viciousness entering his voice.

'Your name is not Dylan Shumack. It's David Stacey. It was you Jeff Ottway called me about. It was you he hurt all those years ago. It was you he felt so guilty about. He sought forgiveness, and you denied him that.'

'I don't know what you're talking about,' said the man in the wheelchair, but he said it faintly, and it lacked conviction.

'Establishing identity is an easy thing to do. I won't even have to bring your mother from her nursing home to do it. Whatever you're calling yourself here in this building, your real name will be on your driver's licence. You are David Stacey.'

There was a long, heavy silence, which, at last, the young man broke.

'Okay. Okay. I'm David Stacey. So what? What does that prove?'

'It proves that you came here under false pretences. That you've been pretending all along. Pretending to me. Pretending to the police.'

'And why shouldn't I?' He was becoming aggressive now. 'It's none of your business, and no business of the police either.'

'If you killed Jeff Ottway, it is.'

'But I didn't! And you can't prove I did, either!'

'I can show that you have motive . . .' began Roman.

'Show me then!' interrupted Shumack/Stacey.

'It was Jeff Ottway who drove the car that put you into that wheelchair,' Roman said in his low but powerful voice, and the young man shrank back from the sound of it.

'It was early in the morning that the accident happened. You were out jogging. Was Jeff coming home from an all-night party? Was he the worse for drink? He hinted at that when he called on my talk-back show the first time. Drunk, he knocked you down. Drunk, he drove off in a panic. That's what happened, isn't it?'

David Stacey, 'Dylan Shumack' glared at Roman. There was a mixture of pain and anger in his eyes.

'You idolised him. It was bad enough to be made a paraplegic. But to know that your best friend, your hero, had crippled you—and then driven off and left you to be found by a milkman on his early morning run. That must have been a pain almost too great to bear.'

'It's a pain that never ends,' said Stacey, quietly and bitterly. 'It's inside all the time, every minute of the day.'

'Exactly. When did you discover that Ottway was the driver who had knocked you down? He never visited you in hospital—of course he couldn't, he couldn't face you. He was already being tortured by guilt over what he had done. You confronted him when you came out of hospital. You were upset that he hadn't visited you. Is that when he confessed? Told you that he had driven the car?'

Very softly, so that Roman had to strain to hear, Stacey said, 'Yes . . . that's when he told me.'

'And you hated him, didn't you?' resumed Roman. 'Not with a loud, hot anger—but with a cold, poisonous anger that was determined he would suffer for as long as you suffered. You took the joy out of his wedding day just by turning up. Or did you do more? Did you take him to one side and tell him you could never marry—that he had destroyed that side of your life, too? Is that what you did? For as long as he lived in the Ramsgate area he kept seeing you around—you would have made sure of that. You worked on his guilt, didn't you? You made him feel it, didn't you?'

'Yes, I did,' said Stacey, defiant now. 'And why shouldn't I? After what he did to me. I decided that he should share my suffering—every single day of it. I used to make sure that he caught glimpses of me all the time—outside of Bright's, where I used to work with him, outside the flat where he lived with Lesley. When I knew he was looking I used to struggle to do things and deliberately fail. Things like getting up and down gutters or steps. I didn't say anything, I just made him look at me—look at what he had done.'

'And that gave him nightmares,' completed Roman.

'Did it?' said Stacey. 'I didn't know that.'

'It made him sullen and withdrawn. It broke up his first marriage.'

'Good!' hissed Stacey, spitting out the word. 'Did you know that at one stage Lesley lost interest in Jeff? Well, she did. And I think she started to fancy me. But then Jeff made me a cripple—and that was the end of that. He put me through hell—and I made him pay for it.'

'Have you ever asked yourself why?' Roman said gently.

'Why what?'

'Why other paraplegics cope so much better than you. People like Meg Palmer upstairs. She's pregnant now, did you know that? It was a car accident that put her in a chair, but she has forgiven and put all that behind her. Her life is rich and full.'

'I know what you're full of . . .' interrupted Stacey.

Roman ploughed on, ignoring the interruption,

'Who did you *really* hurt with your refusal to forgive? Jeff Ottway? Or yourself?'

'Don't be stupid! I had my knife into Jeff—and I twisted it. It was great! He deserved it.'

'But then Jeff disappeared from Rockdale, didn't he?'

'Ran away from me, that's what he did.'

'That's right. He couldn't cope with seeing you around, so he moved. And what did you do?'

'Me? I waited. I wasn't going to give up on my revenge. I thought about him almost every day. I knew I'd see him again.'

'Your father died, your mother moved into a nursing home, and you stayed on in the family home in Rockdale, waiting . . . waiting for what?'

'For a chance to find out where Jeff had moved to.'

'And you waited how long? Ten years?'

'Twelve. But I'm a good hater. And good haters know how to wait.'

'How did you find him in the end?'

'I was driving past his parents' place one afternoon when I saw Jeff and a woman and child getting into a car. I followed them. All the way across Sydney. All the way to this block of units.'

Roman stood up. His height and bulk blocked out most of the light from the window. He seemed to make the room shrink around him. 'And then what did you do?' he asked.

'I investigated. I found out that this block had a lift, and a ramp and so on, and that meant I could live here in my wheelchair. So then I rang up real estate agents and told them I wanted to buy an apartment in this block—just this block and no

178

other. When one became vacant I was lucky—it was on the same floor as Jeff.'

'So you moved in?'

'Yes.'

'Did Jeff recognise you?'

'No. He never gave me a second glance.'

'Because your appearance had changed,' rumbled Roman. 'The skinny kid he once knew had put on a lot of weight, had ballooned out.'

'It's sitting around in this chair all day that does it!'

'No, it's self-indulgence that does it. Living on Coke and Mars Bars. It hasn't happened to Meg Palmer, has it?'

Stacey said nothing, so Roman continued, 'When did you identify yourself to Jeff? When did he discover who you really were?'

'Just two weeks ago,' Stacey chuckled maliciously at the memory. 'It was a real shock, I can tell you.'

'And then when Caitlin and Eleanor went away to visit Caitlin's parents, Jeff took the opportunity to call me on the show and ask for advice. As a result of which, he came and apologised to you.'

'That was good, that was,' snorted Stacey. 'I led him on for a while—made him lay it on thick—got him thinking that I might accept his apology and let him off the hook. Then I threw it back in his face.'

'Jeff described you as "vicious."'

'Well, I had a right to be,' Stacey said, just for a moment sounding defensive.

'The Neelys heard the sounds of an argument that afternoon. But because the argument was heard coming from your apartment, not Jeff's, I didn't understand the significance of it for a long time.'

'You think you're so smart, don't you, Roman? Well, answer one question—just to settle my curiosity. How did you work out that I was David Stacey?'

'It was partly a matter of elimination. There wasn't much in Jeff's past that he could have been referring to when he talked about his haunting guilt. After I'd talked to Peter O'Neil's sister, I was convinced that it had to have something to do with the hit and run accident to David Stacey. And here you were, right on spot, with exactly the right sort of disability. So I suspected it. And then you confirmed it for me.'

'How?'

'When you rang my show to talk about the Rockdale pool—the way it was years ago.'

'The monkeys?'

'Yes, you rang to remind me about the monkeys. And that told me that you were an old Rockdale boy—and two of the important pieces of the jigsaw puzzle fitted together.'

'Alright. Alright,' Stacey said, 'You're clever, I'll give you that. And I don't deny that I hated Ottway. But I didn't kill him—I swear that I didn't.'

'I just wish I could believe you, David,' said Roman with utter conviction. 'I wish I could—but I can't.'

'Why would I want him dead? I was enjoying tormenting him!'

'No you weren't. That's the whole point. The tormenting game had satisfied you years before, but now it had lost its edge. After years of poisonous brooding you could be satisfied with nothing less than Jeff Ottway's death.'

'Listen! You don't seem to realise that I *couldn't* have done the murder . . . physical impossibility! That copper who came to see me . . . ah . . .'

'McDermott?'

'That's him, McDermott. He told me that Jeff had been hit on the back of the head by someone who was taller and stronger than him. I can't get out of this chair, Roman! Or do you think I'm faking it?'

'No, you're not faking it—your paraplegia is quite real.'

'So, I couldn't be the killer, right?'

'That's what had me baffled for such a long time. But now I understand. All the rest of the pieces of the puzzle have fallen into place. It was the sounds that pointed me in the right direction.'

'What sounds?'

'Those people in the building who heard anything at all during the hour when the murder was committed reported hearing the same things.'

'What things?'

'Things like cars in the garage, the lift operating, people moving about. Perfectly normal sounds— no-one thought anything about them. But they started me thinking about what had really happened that night. Because what they heard was *you*, David—opening and closing the boot of your car, using the lift, moving along the corridor.'

'You're making this up. You don't know anything.' But for once Stacey sounded afraid.

'Meg Palmer has been trying to help you, hasn't she?'

'So what? She's a do-gooder, that's all!'

'What do you want people to be?' snapped Roman. 'Do-badders? Of course she's a do-gooder . . . she was trying to help you.'

'I'm not denying that,' Stacey said with a shrug of his shoulders.

'She wanted to lift you out of your self-pity by giving you a sense of responsibility. With that in mind she asked you to keep an eye on their apartment while she and Jason were in Vanuatu. In other words, you had a key to the Palmers' apartment.'

Stacey just swallowed hard.

'You went up there while the Palmers were away. I saw the black rubber marks from the tyres of your wheelchair on the skirting boards in their apartment.'

'But they might have been . . .'

'They might have been from Meg's wheelchair, but they weren't. They were there the moment Meg and Jason entered the apartment from their holidays. I know—I was there, and I saw the marks. And Meg would not have gone on holidays leaving such marks behind—she is fanatical about keeping the place spotlessly clean. So—you were there.'

Stacey remained silent, as Roman continued.

'On the night of the murder, you were in the Palmers' apartment, directly above Jeff's. When Jeff stepped out onto the lawn for a cigarette, after talking to me, you leaned over the balcony and dropped—what was it? A spanner? A tyre lever?— onto his skull. The blow killed him instantly. That's how you did it. It wasn't physically impossible at all. Do you want to tell me the rest, David—or shall I go on telling you?'

Stacey started to twist and shift uncomfortably in his wheelchair. But he couldn't take his eyes off the large, brooding figure of Roman.

'Nothing to say? Then I'll continue, shall I? What did you do after the murder? Well, obviously you came down in the lift and moved the body. You couldn't have got in through the front door of Jeff's apartment. So you must have gone around the outside of the building to where Jeff was lying, dead, on the grass, and moved him in through the patio door—which was standing wide open at the time. How did you move him? I don't know, but I'm prepared to guess. Perhaps you lashed a piece of rope around his feet and towed him the short distance across the lawn and into his own lounge room.'

Stacey managed to drag his eyes away from the hypnotic figure of Mark Roman, and he stared down at his hands in his lap.

'You are very clever with that chair of yours, and you have very powerful arms. So I'm guessing that's how you moved the body. And the result was three bloodstains: the one on the carpet under Jeff's body, the long smear on the carpet where he had been dragged, and the third stain—the dried blood that I found on the grass, marking the spot where he had actually died. Then you closed the patio door, turned out the lights, and let yourself out of Jeff's front door, taking the murder weapon with you. But you didn't pull Jeff's door properly closed when you left, which is why it swung open when I knocked on it the next morning. Have I left anything out?'

Stacey continued to look down at his hands.

'Where is the murder weapon, David? Did you

return it to the boot of your car? Is it still there for the police to find?'

Stacey looked up at him sharply.

'You should have disposed of it, David. It wasn't wise to keep it.'

'So what are you going to do now?' asked Stacey quietly.

'What can I do? I have to tell the police, David. I have no choice.'

'You'll never prove it,' Stacey said, a hard edge creeping into his voice. 'When the police come I'll simply deny it. If they charge me, I'll plead not guilty. I'll protest my innocence. I'll hire the best defence lawyer. They'll never make it stick. There's no evidence. I'm quite safe.'

'So you admit it then?' rumbled Roman.

'Oh yes, I admit it. I admit it all. You've got it quite right, Mr Roman. Very clever of you. But that's just between us—from now on, I'm denying everything. Go and fetch the cops. Do whatever you want. I'm ready for you.'

A few moments later Roman was driving towards the Chatswood Police Station, tense and anxious.

'May I see Detective Marsh, please?' said Roman, at the reception desk. They kept him waiting for several minutes, then Marsh appeared.

'You wanted to see me, Mr Roman? What about? How can I help you?'

'Jeff Ottway was murdered by David Stacey,' said Roman bluntly.

'David . . . who?'

'Stacey. He's living in the apartment block under the name of "Dylan Shumack."'

'Ah, yes. He's on our list as a witness. McDermott spoke to him. Well, thank you for your suggestion, Mr Roman. Now, if you'd like to leave us to get on with our job . . .'

'He has just admitted it to me,' Roman interrupted. 'And the murder weapon is still in his car in the basement.'

'If this is a wind-up, Roman . . .' threatened Marsh.

'It's not.' And Roman's tone of voice convinced the detective.

'Alright. Tell me about it in the car.'

Two minutes later Roman, Marsh and McDermott were speeding back towards Cambridge Street, followed by two uniformed officers in a patrol car.

At the front security door Marsh pressed the buzzer marked 'Shumack.' There was no response.

'Mr Shumack. This is Detective Marsh. Open up please, sir,' said Marsh, speaking into the intercom set into the wall. Still there was no response.

'This is great Roman!' said McDermott. 'How do you propose we get in now?'

'I'll do it,' said Roman, pressing the buzzer marked 'Neely.'

'Hello, Jayne? It's Mark again. Would you let me in please?'

'Yes, of course, Mark,' her voice crackled over the intercom as the front door unlocked.

The group strode purposefully across the lobby, past a startled Jayne Neely, and pounded on the door of the apartment belonging to 'Dylan Shumack.' At first there was no response. Then came the sound of movement inside.

'If you don't open up, Mr Shumack, or Stacey, or whatever your name is—I'll have one of my men break in the door,' bellowed Marsh.

Then they heard it—a loud explosion from inside the apartment.

'Break it down!' yelled Marsh, and McDermott put his shoulder to the door. It gave way with a crunch of splintering wood. Inside the small apartment there was an acrid smell, and wisps of white smoke. They found David Stacey in the lounge room. He had put the barrel of a rifle in his mouth and pulled the trigger. It was not a pretty sight.

Beside him, on the floor, was a scribbled note—a three-line confession—and, wrapped up in a sheet of newspaper, was a bloodstained tyre lever.

Mark Roman didn't do his radio show that night. There was no way he could have. He rang up Tom Mutch, explained what had happened in a few words, and told him to find a substitute for that night. A few minutes later Brian Farrell rang, wanting a voice report from Roman for the news.

'I can't, Brian,' said Roman. 'I'm sorry—I just can't.'

The shock, the depression, the sense of guilt over Stacey's death, froze Roman into a stunned silence. He couldn't articulate how he felt. He found he couldn't articulate anything.

When the police eventually released him, Roman drove to the Rectory at St Thomas' Anglican church, at North Sydney. And when he told Hugh Marsden what had happened, he wept silently.

'The blood of David Stacey is on my hands, Hugh. He's dead because of the way I handled it. There's no way you can deny that.'

'No. I don't think I will deny that. Or, not exactly, anyway. It may well be that you acted unwisely in confronting Stacey rather than taking your story directly to the police. Sure, I understand why you did it. You had good reason, based on recent experience, for believing the police would dismiss out of hand whatever you told them. So I understand why you did it. But that doesn't necessarily make it wise.'

'This is a death of which I am guilty,' muttered Roman bitterly.

'Well, that statement I can't agree with. When someone commits suicide—anyone, David Stacey or anyone else—ultimately it is their own decision to do that. You cannot take someone else's action and make yourself responsible for it.'

Roman nodded, hearing what Hugh was saying, but not wanting to accept it.

'And remember, the real damage had been done to David Stacey years before—by himself, not by Jeff Ottway or anyone else. Stacey was crippled alright, but he was crippled *inside*, because he had chosen to hug his hatred and his refusal to forgive in his heart. And the result was that his heart became poisoned and withered. The seeds of his death lay there—rather than in your action. Stacey's death, ultimately, sprang from the same seed as Jeff Ottway's death. Namely, from Stacey's dangerous self-obsession, which, in his case, took the form of self-pity.'

'I can understand all that,' Roman murmured quietly, 'but I still *feel* guilty.'

'That's the emotional shock you've been through. Of course you'll feel that way. But the solution is to bring your *feeling* under the control of your *thinking*. You are a Christian. You are someone who has turned from your way of living to God's way. Years ago you asked God to come into your life and take charge of your life. You did

187

that because you realised that you were cut off from God, that you had offended Him, and that you needed to be forgiven and changed. You placed yourself in His hands. You were able to do that because Jesus brought you and God together. In his death on the Cross Jesus paid for all the damage you have done in your life—including something as big and shocking as the death of David Stacey. That is why Jesus is the only one qualified to rescue us and forgive us.'

Roman put down his coffee cup, and, groping for his handkerchief, dabbed at his eyes. They were not tears of sorrow this time, but tears of wonder, of gratitude, at the enormity of the God who forgives.